FLORIDA STATE
UNIVERSITY LIBRARIES

MAY 1 0 2001

TALLAHASSEE, FLORIDA

NORMAN PORTER was born in Belfast in 1952, where he was educated at Methodist College Belfast. In 1970 he and his family emigrated to Australia, where he graduated with a BA in Politics from Flinders University. He holds a D.Phil. in Politics from the University of Oxford, and he later lectured in Politics at Flinders University. In 1994 he returned to Belfast and joined the Ulster Unionist Party. His frustration with unionist politics prompted him to make a submission to the Forum for Peace and Reconciliation in Dublin and led him to write *Rethinking Unionism* (Blackstaff Press, 1996), which was joint winner of the 1997 Christopher Ewart-Biggs Memorial Prize. He is married with three children.

# The Republican Ideal

## Current Perspectives

*edited and with an introduction by*
**Norman Porter**

THE
BLACKSTAFF
PRESS

BELFAST

ACKNOWLEDGEMENTS

I am very grateful to the Northern Ireland Voluntary Trust for financial support which made possible the preparation of this book. I am also grateful, again, to the staff at Blackstaff Press for their customary professionalism, efficiency and goodwill.

First published in 1998 by
The Blackstaff Press Limited
3 Galway Park, Dundonald, Belfast BT16 2AN, Northern Ireland
This book has received support from the
Cultural Diversity Programme of the Community Relations Council,
which aims to encourage acceptance and understanding of cultural diversity.
The views expressed do not necessarily reflect those of the
NI Community Relations Council.

© Selection and Introduction, Norman Porter, 1998
© The contributors, 1998
All rights reserved

The contributors have asserted their right under the
Copyright, Designs and Patents Act 1988 to be identified as
the authors of this work.

Typeset by Techniset Typesetters, Newton-le-Willows, Merseyside

Printed in England by Biddles Limited

A CIP catalogue record for this book
is available from the British Library

ISBN 0-85640-627-9

# Contents

1 INTRODUCTION
  The Republican Ideal and Its Interpretations ... 1
  NORMAN PORTER

2 The Republican Ideal Regained ... 34
  MARTIN MANSERGH

3 The Republican Ideal ... 62
  MITCHEL McLAUGHLIN

4 The Concept of Republicanism ... 85
  DES O'HAGAN

5 Reclaiming Republicanism ... 113
  EAMON HANNA

6 Pluralism and the Death of Deference ... 132
  DAVID COOK

7 Republicanism Revisited ... 156
  AVILA KILMURRAY AND MONICA McWILLIAMS

  NOTES ON THE CONTRIBUTORS ... 170

  INDEX ... 171

# 1

# Introduction
# The Republican Ideal and Its Interpretations

NORMAN PORTER

Republicanism inspires. And it terrifies. Maybe it no longer does both in most Western societies. But it does in Northern Ireland. To compound difficulties here, those whom republicanism inspires seem pretty poor at relieving the fears of those whom it terrifies. Or, perhaps more accurately, the terrified appear to have little interest in hearing from the inspired. Either way a serious communication problem exists which, in addition to its wider political ramifications, impedes understanding of republicanism.

A generation of politically motivated violence in the North – frequently conducted either by or against republicans – helps explain why such an unfortunate situation prevails. Under conditions of violence or its threat, it is not difficult to see how one group's source of political meaning becomes another group's bogey, or how contrasting attitudes to republicanism may harden to the point where they appear virtually inaccessible to reasonable interchange. Recent events in Northern Ireland – most notably the prospect of a new political dispensation emerging from the successful conclusion of multi-party talks at Stormont, overwhelmingly endorsed by a referendum – hint that this unfortunate situation may not always be our lot. But that is to project too far into the future.

At the moment we still have to deal with a communication breakdown between many republicans and their opponents which exacerbates misunderstanding of what republicanism stands for. If it is unfair to blame republicans for continuing failures of communication, it is not unreasonable to suggest that various of them share responsibility for the distortions of republicanism entertained by many unionists in particular. For example, those whose activities encourage the impression that republicanism simply signifies the sort of commitment to a united Ireland that requires the use of armed force merely confirm unionism's worst prejudices. Indeed, it is precisely this impression that serves the polemical purposes of certain unionists who, in also observing that republican commitment is found mainly among Catholics, proceed to peddle republicanism's ultimate distortion: its reduction to a synonym of violent, sectarian nationalism.

This distortion is galling. There is nothing about republicanism as a political philosophy that intrinsically connects it to violence, whatever the actions of some of its adherents. As we shall see, the putative identification of nationalism and republicanism is much more contentious than is often supposed. And sectarianism is inimical to any republican ideal worthy of the name. Stressing these points is essential if republicanism is to be opened up to meaningful debate. Having to stress them, however, perhaps indicates the difficulties republicans face in convincing doubters that they represent much more than an exclusive and insular political standpoint. There is an irony here, given Irish republicanism's eighteenth-century origins. Whatever else may be said about the United Irishmen, there is little doubt that they stood for an inclusive and open-minded political creed. Their republicanism anticipated the transcendence of religious divisions in political affairs, it was inspired by the ideas of the American and French revolutions and, more generally, it reflected the ethos of the Enlightenment. Two hundred years on from the United Irishmen's unsuccessful rebellion against English rule in Ireland, it is especially appropriate to revisit the republican ideal and explore what it still has to offer beyond the distortions of its more virulent critics.

APPROACHES AND UNDERSTANDINGS

This volume of essays contributes to such revisiting and exploration by taking as its overarching theme the question of the republican ideal's pertinence today. The contributors are political activists drawn from six political parties, North and South. Three of the parties represented – Fianna Fáil, Sinn Féin, and the Workers' Party – explicitly define themselves as republican, whereas the three others – the Social Democratic and Labour Party (SDLP), the Alliance Party of Northern Ireland, and the Northern Ireland Women's Coalition – do not, although it is probably true to say that many members of the SDLP in particular happily describe themselves as constitutional republicans. Each contributor offers his or her individual angle on republicanism, rather than a party line, but it is worth adding that none of those from the republican parties, namely Martin Mansergh, Mitchel McLaughlin and Des O'Hagan, risk expulsion for anything they have written here. As the remaining contributors – Eamon Hanna, David Cook, Avila Kilmurray and Monica McWilliams – are writing in purely personal capacities, it is unlikely that they will incur any official party displeasure either.

A feature of all of the contributions is that they support some version of the republican ideal Since none of them supposes that current Irish or British political life adequately satisfies the requirements of such an ideal, an anticipatory strain is present in their analyses. They look forward to a time when republican values may more thoroughly inform political practice. The implicit – and in instances explicit – claim of the following chapters is that the republican ideal provides a crucial set of standards which, if adopted by enough of us, would improve our politics, North and South. This claim underscores a point worth highlighting, namely that this is a book written by advocates rather than by commentators. It does not so much offer discussions *about* republicanism, as facilitate cases *for* the republican ideal. This may make it an exercise of doubtful value to those readers who have become accustomed to think of disinterested commentators as the political sages of our time. Here the remarks of the North American philosopher Hubert Dreyfus and his colleagues are germane, when they aver that commentators 'who have a view on every issue but have not taken a stand on any ... lack the passionate perspective which can lead to risk of serious error and therefore also to wisdom'.[1] In this context, this is another way of saying that the voices most worth listening to, and engaging with, if we wish to grasp what republicanism is about are those devoted to its cause.

The voices represented in this volume are not singing from the same song sheet, however. Although various of them raise common concerns, they reflect different approaches to, and understandings of, the republican ideal. On occasion, matters of difference are given direct and sharp expression: through Hanna's rejection of the legitimacy of militant republicanism, say, or through O'Hagan's critique of the republican credentials of Sinn Féin. For the most part, though, the differences among the contributors appear more indirectly.

The indirectness of their appearance should not of course be mistaken for unimportance. Significant differences of approach, focus and political priority are evident. All the essays include some historical component – with the experiences of the United Irishmen providing a common reference point that is used to facilitate the telling of sometimes dissimilar stories – but some are more specifically historical than others in their mode of analysis. Ideological and party interests dictate the approach of certain essays but are much less discernible in others. One essay discloses a lot of biographical detail and the others virtually none. The focus of the essays varies too. Attention may be fixed primarily on the island of Ireland as a whole, or more emphasis may be put on affairs in the South, or in the North, or even in the UK in general. Most crucially, opinions diverge over what the republican ideal chiefly consists in, over which political priorities it entails. The essays identify variously three main priorities as being warranted by the ideal: resolution of the national question through moves to end the partition of Ireland, commitment to a particular form of government, and dedication to transforming the character of society. Some contributors are anxious to affirm all three of these, but others are not. And even where agreement exists on a priority, it is common to find disagreement about its meaning.

These sorts of difference of approach, focus and understanding make for a varied, if not eclectic, collection of essays. The collection's sheer diversity serves two valuable purposes. First, it underscores the contestability of all versions of republicanism. At the very least, it should now be difficult for any particular person, group or party to presume a monopoly of republican wisdom. This is not to imply that there are not better and worse, or more plausible and less plausible, conceptions of the republican ideal. But it is to say that all conceptions are disputable and are required to prove their worth through reasoned argument. Second, the range of opinion on display here seriously discredits the caricatures of republicanism propagated by many of its opponents. In doing so, it may show why there are good reasons for encouraging ongoing debate not only among republicans, but also between republicans of all hues and their critics.

Now let me say something more specific about each contribution. The opening essay by Martin Mansergh of Fianna Fáil combines a broad historical imagination with a detailed grasp of the nuances of Irish politics, especially in the South. Mansergh provides a snapshot of the development of republicanism from its origins in the ancient Greek city-state through to its acceptance as the constitutional norm in Europe following World War One. In the course of attending to its fate within Ireland, he reminds us of two fascinating points that are often overlooked: that Cromwellians were the first republicans in Ireland and that, given the nature of the republicanism of the United Irishmen, it is more than a little ironic that most republicans now are drawn from Catholic backgrounds whereas most Protestants define themselves as loyalists or unionists. Mansergh identifies various strands within Irish republicanism since the 1790s, including the secular, the separatist and the constitutional. For Mansergh, the best expression of the republican ideal is found within the constitutional strand that evolved in the South, not least through the efforts of Eamon de Valera. Constitutional republicanism, he tells us, is associated with 'a proud, self-respecting and modern Irish nationalism'. This is a nationalism that spurns irredentism and that thus eschews separatist republicanism and its appeals to armed struggle to advance republican goals. In recent years, constitutional republicanism has acquired at least three characteristics. One is a tactical commitment to the development of a nationalist consensus – mainly involving the Irish government, the SDLP and Sinn Féin – to underscore that republican and nationalist goals should be pursued by peaceful and democratic means only. Another is a principled recognition that constitutional disputes between North and South must be settled by an agreement that respects the principles of self-determination and consent. A third characteristic is constitutional republicanism's commitment to the maintenance of a democratic and pluralist society capable of accommodating the identities of all citizens.

Mitchel McLaughlin of Sinn Féin in his essay investigates a number of facets of the United Irishmen's experience and identifies strongly with what he sees as the egalitarian impulse that underlay their actions and beliefs. He charts a brief history of the republican movement since 1798. The partition of Ireland in

1921 looms large on his horizon as a defining moment for republicanism. Not only did partition violate the Irish people's right to self-determination, he maintains, but it also precipitated civil war in the South and an intensification of sectarianism in the North. Within the North, under unionist rule at Stormont, nationalists and republicans were treated as second-class citizens. McLaughlin gives a quick account of some important developments in the attitude of Sinn Féin to politics in the North especially. Considerable emphasis is placed on the role the party has played in the peace process, including its commitment to the nationalist consensus that Mansergh mentions. Three points, with obvious tactical ramifications, are worth picking out of his account. First, McLaughlin attributes significance to Britain's declared lack of any selfish strategic or economic interests in Ireland. Persuading Britain that it should no longer have any political interest in the North seems to him the obvious next step, given the path upon which it has already embarked. Second, he recognises the reality of unionists' British identity and tries to provide assurances that such an identity has nothing to fear in the sort of all-Ireland arrangements he envisages. These are arrangements, third, that are guided by the egalitarian spirit prevalent among the United Irishmen. Importantly, McLaughlin thinks these arrangements should be attended to now rather than postponed until the ending of partition. Accordingly, an equality agenda assumes an immediate importance for life within northern and southern societies. It is this that provides the key, he argues, for overcoming such social problems as coercion, discrimination, oppression, intolerance and prejudice. Moves should be made instantly, he advises, to create a pluralist society that safeguards individual and group rights, affords equal economic opportunities, accommodates diverse cultural expressions, and enjoys an impartial legal system.

Des O'Hagan takes as his point of departure the emergence and development of the Workers' Party, which he regards as the authentic heir of the United Irishmen's brand of republicanism and of the progressive radical stream within the republican movement in the 1930s. Unlike Mansergh and McLaughlin who link republican and nationalist interests, he is dismissive of any connection between republicanism and nationalism. Although he shares their aspiration for a united Ireland, this is for him neither a matter of nationalist conviction nor an overriding political priority. What counts more, in his opinion, is creating societies, North and South, that are free from clerical and sectarian influence, societies that are based upon democratic principles and organised along socialist lines. According to O'Hagan, nationalism poses one of the major obstacles to the creation of such societies in Ireland. Not only is nationalism responsible for wreaking social and political havoc in other parts of the world but, he contends, it is responsible for maintaining sectarian practices within Northern Ireland. Sinn Féin, he claims, has embraced nationalism rather too enthusiastically and, as a consequence, has lost sight of the revolutionary dimension of republicanism. The actions of the Provisional IRA have, in his opinion, been counter-revolutionary. In O'Hagan's view, the tragedy is that the United Irishmen's hope of uniting 'Protestant, Catholic and Dissenter', which for him now means above all else the achievement of working-class unity, has been sacrificed for spurious ends. For him, defending a conception of the republican ideal that incorporates international, democratic, secular and socialist aspects is the principal priority. And struggling to recapture the ground lost by this conception through a generation of sectarian violence is assumed to be republicanism's most urgent task.

The essay by Eamon Hanna of the SDLP distinguishes itself in terms of the biographical detail he provides in its second part. In the first part, he concentrates his discussion on the United Irishmen and what we may profitably glean from their example. What emerges from his analysis is a conception of republicanism as a non-sectarian, democratic and inclusive political ideal, an ideal with the potential to change various of our practices and attitudes within Northern Ireland. He laments that much that currently passes for republicanism lacks the complexities and subtleties of the United Irishmen's thought. And he finds a salutary lesson in the fact that their opposition to English rule in Ireland during the eighteenth century was not fuelled by any hatred of the English as such. His essay indicates that republicanism must acknowledge that there is a difference in kind between the nature of the British presence in Ireland that the United Irishmen fought against and that which exists now within Northern Ireland. Adequate acknowledgement of such a difference, he thinks, entails treating the principles of separatism and national sovereignty as rather less than immutable. Otherwise, considerable disservice is done to the republican ideal and the prospects of us overcoming our most serious divisions in the North are gloomy.

David Cook of the Alliance Party takes a very different tack from the others, by focusing more on Britain than on Ireland. His essay embarks upon a voyage beginning in the thirteenth century, when limitations were imposed on the exercise of kingly rule through the signing of Magna Carta in 1215. Cook tells a story that highlights subsequent episodes in English, Irish, North American and European history that helped to claw back power from the monarchy and to increase the rights entitled to citizens. Even if we do not quite require another episode of epoch-making significance, he maintains that British society would benefit enormously from a more thorough embrace of republican insights, since it is these that make an invaluable contribution to the development of a fully pluralist state. And it is achievement of such a state that Cook regards as the ultimate political aim, that is, a state based on principles of justice and equality with social and political structures that facilitate and respect citizens' diversity. This state does not necessarily entail abolition of a hereditary head of state, but it does imply a demystification of the monarchy, an entirely ceremonial definition of its duties, a desectarianisation of its constitutional position, and an end to all deferential customs and practices. The essence of republicanism, for Cook, consists not so much in being against monarchy, or at least not a constitutional monarchy, as in being insistent that power resides in the body of citizens. And it is through a proper recognition of citizen power that he thinks the pluralist state he envisages becomes possible.

In their essay, Avila Kilmurray and Monica McWilliams of the Northern Ireland Women's Coalition ask whether republicanism is an end in itself, whether it can be separated from nationalism, and whether there is value in a concept of civic republicanism. These questions are set against a historical background that considers the development of republicanism in Ireland since the United Irishmen. For Kilmurray and McWilliams, republicanism was too quickly put to the service of nationalist ends and, as a consequence, became alien to what they call the 'British Ulster tradition'. For them, republicanism needs disentangling from nationalism, and the best way for this to occur is through recapturing and reworking the civic republican strand evident in the thought of the United Irishmen. Civic republicanism has the potential to include all traditions in Ireland, and it emphasises the importance of an active citizenry. Its agenda envisages a society that is not only egalitarian but also permits difference to flourish. According to Kilmurray and McWilliams, important lessons for the shaping of such a society, whether North or South, can be learned from the women's movement. Special attention should be paid to the concerns of groups at the margins of the political process, they think, and security should be guaranteed to individuals and to minorities within society, North and South. In sum, what is needed, they argue, is an update of Wolfe Tone's vision of the unity of 'Protestant, Catholic and Dissenter' that sees the various communities and identities in Ireland uniting in their quest for a common good that takes seriously the issues of equity, inclusion and human rights.

Any number of queries are prompted by the views expressed in each of these essays. Among the more interesting are those that ask hard questions of the political priorities associated with the republican ideal. I want to suggest two lines of probing these priorities that raise issues very much worth arguing about. One relates to an aspect of the national question. Specifically, I ask about the relationship between republicanism and nationalism which, in this volume at least, seems more problematic than is popularly assumed. Since the questions involved in probing this relationship are highly controversial, I devote most of what follows to exploring them. A second line, which I deal with more briefly, focuses on the sort of society that features in republican analyses and, in particular, on what such a society means for citizens.

REPUBLICANISM AND NATIONALISM

Settling the national question by bringing an end to partition in Ireland is probably what many people think Irish republicanism stands for. It is hardly an exaggeration to say that Ireland's full independence from Britain – which is what partition's termination is intended to achieve – has for long been perceived as the dominant aspiration of the republican movement. And it is precisely this aspiration that republicans share with nationalists in Ireland. To reduce republicanism to the quest for national independence is, however, limiting. In fairness, this is admitted by contributors to this volume who rate the quest highly, since they too argue that republicanism stands for other things besides. But it is the tendency of these other things to be sidelined for the sake of national unity and independence that concerns a number of contributors. So much so, indeed, that some of them imply that the republican ideal is diminished by its identification with moves to abolish partition.

Different reasons explain their unease. Sifting through the essays of Cook, Hanna, Kilmurray and McWilliams, and O'Hagan at least four reasons are discernible. The identification disturbs (1) because Northern Ireland's place within the United Kingdom is valued and the privileging of Irish unity and independence discounts the possibility of being republican and unionist; or (2) because preoccupation with the national question in practice encourages violence and a purist attitude that is ill equipped to display the flexibility successful politics requires; or (3) because the topic of the North's constitutional future is a matter of relative indifference which, if prioritised, impedes other types of political development; or (4) because the case for Ireland's reunification frequently appears in terms that involve republicanism's collapse into nationalism and, in doing so, stultifies the advancement of republicans' proper interests. Each of these reasons, in cautioning against an overemphasis on the national question, suggests that there is something worrying about the way in which republicanism and nationalism tend to be lumped together in Ireland. And it is this suggestion that I want to explore further.

The first reason, which raises the prospect that an individual could be both republican and unionist, runs against the grain of conventional wisdom in Ireland. As baldly stated above, however, it does not rule out any relationship between republicanism and nationalism *per se*. Its objection is to republicanism being regarded exclusively as a brand of *Irish* nationalism. What is kept open is the possibility of republicanism's compatibility with some other brand of nationalism, one, say, with a British orientation. And here it is worth remarking that one of the misleading peculiarities of political language in Northern Ireland is the notion that the only nationalists around are those who aspire to a united Ireland. For its implication that nationalist sentiments of any sort are foreign to unionists is too incredible to be entertained.

The second reason, which shrinks from the extreme measures sometimes employed to pursue national goals, arguing that preoccupation with the national question encourages violence, is not an outright assault on the relationship between republicanism and nationalism either. A moderate expression of the relationship – echoed perhaps in the link Mansergh makes between constitutional republicanism and 'modern' nationalism – remains on the cards. Certainly, the second reason's main target is that rendering of the republican–nationalist nexus that underwrites, or even is ambiguous about, armed struggle as an acceptable means of persuading Britain finally to close its account in Ireland. At its deepest, what is being canvassed is the danger of absolutising the issue of the border, since it allows no leeway to the kind of political negotiations that are essential in a society as divided as the North.

The third reason, which effectively claims agnosticism on the question of Northern Ireland's constitutional position, believing its prioritisation may impede other forms of development, likewise disputes the wisdom of focusing on partition to the point of turning principles of sovereignty, independence and unity into non-negotiable absolutes. But, by inferring that the republican ideal relates to the quality of social and political life within a particular society (whether the North or the South), it constitutes an assault on the republicanism–nationalism relationship in a way that the previous two reasons do not. Here there is little consolation in thinking that republicanism in Ireland may be compatible with more than one kind of nationalism, and small comfort in envisaging a republican–nationalist nexus unsullied by violence and political intransigence. Quite simply, according to this third view, neither of these reformulations guarantee that the republican ideal will not be trumped by nationalist imperatives, however moderately expressed. Of course, should such a guarantee be forthcoming, there is no objection in principle here to a constitutional outcome that favoured Irish nationalism. It is prioritising the efforts to achieve such an outcome that is the problem.

The fourth reason, which inveighs most strongly against any association between republicanism and nationalism, viewing the latter as inimical to republican ideals, obviously shares much in common with the third. But there is an interesting difference between the two: ending the partition of Ireland remains an appropriate republican target on the terms of the fourth. It is not the most important target – making existing northern and southern societies more amenable to anti-sectarian and egalitarian institutions and practices is a higher goal – but it is more than a matter of relative indifference. The challenge is to articulate this point in a vocabulary not already corrupted by nationalism. This is a difficult challenge to meet, given popular perceptions of republicans as a highly motivated group of super-nationalists, whose resolute opposition to partition and unswerving belief in an indivisible Irish nation chide nationalists of weaker conviction and deter them from compromising too much. It is apparently not enough to counteract these perceptions in the manner of Mansergh's marriage of constitutional republicanism and 'modern' nationalism, since this too makes republicanism vulnerable to the playing of a 'green' card. So the message seems to be this: if commitment to a unified Irish state requires an embrace of nationalism then the price of such commitment is too high to pay, as republicans have more pressing tasks to attend to anyway. But the possibility is held out of maintaining this commitment unencumbered by nationalist baggage.

It is clear, then, that the topic of republicanism's relation to nationalism evokes a range of responses. It is also clear that the most acute dividing line is between those who regard a resolution of the national question as republicanism's ultimate objective and those who do not. But if these things are clear, a good deal else remains murky. Our vision starts to fog if we put to one side disputes over how highly the quest to end partition should be ranked, and accept that it figures as a legitimate republican concern in Ireland. For example, as we have noticed, those who are uncomfortable with republicans becoming too closely aligned with Irish nationalists in a bid to achieve a united political entity do not necessarily agree among themselves about the source of their unease. And we have not yet examined whether those who are comfortable with such an alignment – Mansergh and McLaughlin – share similar views on what it should mean. To complicate matters further, there is a suggestion that some version of a republican–nationalist alliance, such as that proposed by Mansergh, may turn out to be acceptable to certain of the doubters. It is not simply a case, in other words, of our contributors dividing neatly into pro-nationalist and anti-nationalist camps. Moreover, there is a lurking suspicion that different sides in the republican debate about nationalism may be (sometimes) talking at cross-purposes. Maybe various of their disagreements are less sharp than they initially appear and merely boil down to differences of emphasis. Then again, maybe certain of their differences are just irreconcilable.

To probe these possibilities, it is useful to ask two questions which may help us to clarify a number of the issues at stake here. Is there a type of nationalism that is utterly incompatible with any intelligible notion of republicanism? And is there another type that is compatible?

It is now tricky to draw the strict distinctions between nationalism and republicanism that were once possible. Prior to the eighteenth century, for example, there was presumed to be a difference in kind between the concept of a 'nation' and that of a 'republic'. The concept of a nation connoted a pre-political entity, as the German philosopher Jürgen Habermas informs us, a concept that was employed to derisive effect by the Romans to identify 'savage', 'barbaric' or 'pagan' peoples. Derision aside, on this understanding, nations 'are communities of people of the same descent, who are integrated geographically, in the form of settlements or neighborhoods, and culturally by their common language, customs and traditions, but who are not yet politically integrated in the form of state organization.'[2] The concept of a republic, by contrast, immediately referred to a political entity highly organised along specific lines. In a republic people were recognised as citizens, as bearers of rights and freedoms, as people afforded opportunities – unavailable to those in a pre-political condition – to cultivate civic virtues.

Such a contrast between a nation and a republic altered with the birth of the modern nation-state, where the cultural factors of language, tradition and so on moved out of the pre-political twilight into the full glare of the political sun. This move has been so decisive that it is now commonplace to think of the nation as the source of state sovereignty, or of the nation as the entity entitled to political self-determination. Indeed, the erosion of the old distinction between a nation and a republic is seemingly so complete that, as Mansergh points out, after World War One republican constitutions became the norm in European nation-states.

On the face of it, then, there now seems nothing exceptional about linking nationalism and republicanism. If the link appears unusual from a British perspective that may only be because Britain is outside the European norm in not having a republican constitution. But to draw only this conclusion is too facile. Not all nationalist expressions are benign. It is hard to imagine how any self-respecting republican would not experience acute discomfort, for instance, with those expressions that tend towards a glorification of the nation or an affirmation of ethnic supremacy. There manifestly are occasions when nationalism and republicanism clash.

The crucial issue in an Irish context is what relation republicanism adopts towards moves to end British rule that are motivated chiefly by nationalist sentiment. During the nineteenth century an Irish nationalism emerged that evoked memory of an ancient Celtic race that pre-existed Ireland's colonisation by England. To recover this memory fully involved advocating a policy of de-Anglicisation, of striving to sever the English link politically and culturally. Later a religious dimension was added to this expression and the image of an Irish nation, Gaelic and Catholic, was a powerful incentive in some quarters to persevere in efforts to persuade Britain to give up its Irish interests. Elements of this image informed the ethos of the southern part of partitioned Ireland, from its inception as the Irish Free State to its emergence as the Irish Republic. Doubtless this ethos influenced the republican movement, with the result that an exclusive and homogeneous notion of cultural nationalism was regarded by some as integral to the republican project. But this notion sits uneasily with republicanism in two major senses.

First, it is scarcely true to a republican heritage that traces its roots back to the United Irishmen. Tone's vision of unifying 'Protestant, Catholic and Dissenter' under the 'common name of Irishman' implies a nationality that is not tied to one creed or one ethnic stock. Irish cultural nationalism's corruption of the republican ideal of the United Irishmen is unambiguous here. Second, such cultural nationalism contradicts what I understand to be a fundamental tenet of republicanism: the requirement that the public institutions and practices of a society are owned by all of its citizens, that the public ethos of a society is one that all citizens recognise as theirs. Quite simply, the South, at least prior to its entry into Europe, failed to satisfy this requirement. Of course, there may be all sorts of historical and prudential reasons why an ethos alien to unionism and Protestantism prevailed, but they weren't republican reasons. What republicanism in Ireland played on, however, was the anti-colonial spirit it shared with nationalism: both had a common goal of ridding Irish society of foreign influences that were perceived as a source of their centuries-old domination and oppression. Unionists were presumed to be mere lackeys of a colonial power, a group who did not possess an identity worth taking seriously in its own right.

Nobody in this volume plays a cultural nationalist card in this fashion. Irredentism is now dead according to Mansergh and, he stresses, the South has developed into a pluralist society in step with liberal democratic practices elsewhere in the West. And both McLaughlin and he invoke the anti-sectarian ideal of the United Irishmen as very much their own. Most current republicans and nationalists, it seems, have abandoned the strident exclusivism of cultural nationalism and have replaced it with a welcoming inclusivism anxious to respect and accommodate a British identity within a new Ireland. Accordingly, all contributors to this volume appear to be speaking with one voice to the extent that none assumes that all types of Irish nationalism are compatible with the republican ideal.

There may remain, however, a tactical divergence between the contributors, which arguably betrays a difference of some consequence. Anti-nationalist republican voices are much more inclined than others to point to uncomfortable features of republicanism's entanglement with cultural nationalism, and to highlight the obstacles these continue to pose to the overcoming of sectarianism in the North. Their claim is that if we are to be faithful to the United Irishmen's anti-sectarian project, there is an onus on republicans explicitly to denounce the cultural nationalism that equated 'true' Irishness with Gaelicism and Catholicism, and to distance themselves from its residual traces within nationalist culture. Their hunch is that whilst other republicans may no longer promote such a nationalist outlook, they have been prepared to work with it for the sake of ending partition. And, it is hinted, pro-nationalist republicans are still not beyond manipulating exclusivist nationalist tendencies for political advantage. But, for anti-nationalists, this is to compromise republicanism; it is to condemn republicanism in the eyes of Protestants, it is to invert republicanism's proper priorities. So even where differences between republicans on the question of nationalism appear most amenable to reconciliation, thorny difficulties still remain.

If there are nationalist expressions that embarrass most contemporary republicans, even if some are more reticent than others in advertising this fact, are there other expressions of nationalism that can be openly embraced? At their simplest, objections to a republican embrace of any sort of nationalism are saying one of two things, if not both: it is wrong in principle and it is unnecessary anyway given the changing political realities of our time. Whether these objections can be sustained unambiguously is a matter of debate.

Take, for instance, one reason for objecting in principle, which essentially consists in a suspicion of all nationalism and is an extension of the point I have just raised about tactical differences between pro-nationalist and anti-nationalist republicans. Even benign nationalism, it is claimed, has the potential to turn ugly and, as experience instructs us, to play the dominant role in any relationship with republicanism. So, if a united Ireland remains a worthy republican goal, this should be advocated using republican arguments only, and all nationalist services should be dispensed with. In Irish terms, this reason confronts the obvious difficulty of underplaying the fact, already noted here, that the United Irishmen's republicanism was connected to an inclusively conceived Irish nationalism. One response to this difficulty, which I think is true to the spirit of O'Hagan's position for example, might run as follows. The United Irishmen tuned into modern nationalism in its infancy and had they witnessed its development they might have taken a more circumspect attitude to it. It is impossible to believe, for instance, that they would have endorsed its de-Anglicising programme in Ireland to the point of jeopardising the secular, anti-sectarian thrust of their own agenda. For them the purpose of ending English rule in Ireland was hardly to replace it with a local alternative reflecting narrow, divisive interests. But the fact that the United Irishmen's republicanism could be usurped by nationalism points to the real problem here: once it is courted, nationalism is difficult to contain. It is better not to court it at all, therefore, even when it appears in its most alluring, benign guise. In short, to overplay the nationalism of the United Irishmen is to miss what is truly significant about their example. And the uncomfortable fact that, despite their increasingly inclusive noises, republican parties do not boast among their membership any significant numbers from Protestant backgrounds bears ample testimony to how far removed we still are from realising anything approximating the United Irishmen's vision, and to the serious damage that nationalism has done to it.

There is some force to such a response which steadfastly refuses to let any nationalism affect obliviousness of its own propensity to perpetuate sectarian divisions in the North. But there remains a question begging an answer: what does a purely republican argument for a united Ireland amount to? Perhaps there is a clue in a strand of the United Irishmen's argument against English rule in Ireland. Their republicanism consists in the conviction that political power is properly the preserve of the people and not of a monarch. Moreover, such power is taken to require for its organisation a republican form of government, where the people are defined as citizens and not as subjects. In the eighteenth-century Irish case, this requirement acquires an additional rub: the achievement of republican goals is seen to demand breaking loose from the colonial domination of English rule.

Adjusting this strand of argument to suit our contemporary circumstances, it is perfectly possible to maintain that the North's achievement of a republican form of government is more likely through its integration with the South than through hoping that constitutional reform in Britain may soon signal the demise of the monarchy. But this is a weak argument which lacks the strength of the United Irishmen's original case. Two factors make all the difference. For a start, as Cook's essay shows, the British monarchy today poses much less of an obstacle to republican aspirations than it did in the latter part of the eighteenth century. Even if the processes of reform in Britain are not about to yield a strictly republican constitution, moves to strip the monarchy of various of its privileges accompanied by moves to devolve power from Westminster arguably contribute to a central republican cause: bringing government more effectively within the reach of citizens. For another thing, the basic thrust of the United Irishmen's case was that English rule dominates. But it is hard to credit that anyone could imagine that the corrupt and arbitrary rule against which the United Irishmen rebelled has any equivalent in contemporary British rule in Northern Ireland. Not only has Britain declared she no longer has any selfish strategic or economic interest in Ireland, but she is willing to facilitate a united Ireland if northern citizens consent to it. And in the meantime she is anxious to devolve powers – which unionists will not be permitted to arrogate to themselves alone – to a proposed new assembly in Northern Ireland. Quite frankly, then, a purely republican argument for a united Ireland no longer cuts the ice it once did. It is not surprising that those who gesture at it do not make Ireland's reunification the ultimate republican priority. Indeed, it is difficult not to believe that a sustained desire to end partition requires the presence of what might be called national or cultural affections.

The mere mention of such affections, however, is enough to worry those who suspect that they might be emphasised to the detriment of republicanism's universal orientation. And it is this worry that points to another principled reason for resisting republicanism's association with any kind of nationalism. Advocates of the universal orientation of republicanism may again resort to the example of the United Irishmen. As the Irish philosopher Richard Kearney points out, their republicanism promoted the enlightened universalism of world citizens. Thus the Manifesto of the Dublin Society of the United Irishmen addressed its readers as 'citizens of the world'.[3] The sense of universalism being invoked here, he explains, 'operated on the assumption that once the antagonisms of embattled religions, languages and races disappeared a new culture of world citizenship would take its place'.[4] But, the argument goes, the experience of republicanism in Ireland once more testifies that it is precisely this aspect of enlightened universalism that loses out once concessions start to be made to national affections.

A problem with this line of thought is not only that, contrary to enlightened expectations, old antagonisms have persisted rather than vanished; it is also that the notion of world citizenship to which the United Irishmen alluded may be too abstract to be meaningful anyway. It may easily appear vulnerable to the objection Michael Walzer makes to any such notion:

> I am not even aware that there is a world such that one could be a citizen of it. No one has ever offered me such citizenship, or described the naturalization process, or enlisted me in the world's institutional structures, or given me an account of its decision procedures (I hope they are democratic), or provided me with a list of the benefits and obligations of citizenship, or shown me the world's calendar and the common celebrations and commemorations of its citizens.[5]

Walzer has a point, inasmuch as a typical understanding of citizenship refers to membership of a particular polity that has its own laws, norms, customs and traditions. Even so, this point should not be allowed to occlude the very important issue of substance that underlies the concern of those who fear that republicanism's universal dimension may be sacrificed at the altar of national affections. Martha Nussbaum captures this issue well in the course of addressing the question of patriotism in the USA: 'to give support to nationalist sentiments subverts, ultimately, even the values that hold a nation together, because it substitutes a colorful idol for the substantive universal values of justice and right'.[6] And it is these values that bind us to our fellow human beings and not just to our fellow nationals.

Now, if we take on board the points both of Walzer and of Nussbaum, the matter to be resolved can be reformulated as follows: how to think of ourselves as citizens of a specific somewhere without letting the sentiments attached to belonging to that somewhere override moral and political standards that ought to apply to citizens everywhere. Or, put in a way that is more attuned to Irish experience, how is it possible to maintain the balance the United Irishmen sought between the universal aspect of their thought and their particular commitments to Ireland?

Given scepticism about the possibility of striking a balance because of nationalism's insatiable appetite, it may be helpful to begin sketching what an answer to this question might look like by drawing a conceptual distinction between 'nationalism' and 'nationality'. Teasing out some earlier references, by 'nationalism' I mean here an ideology with inclinations towards homogeneity that make membership of a nation a prerogative of those sharing similar characteristics of, say, race, religion or language; an ideology with totalising tendencies that seek to make all other commitments subservient to commitment to the nation; an ideology with insular instincts that oppose any dilution of the purity of a nation's culture through the infiltration of 'foreign' influences; an ideology, finally, with an inherently exclusive bent which treats those not in possession of the nation's defining characteristics but living within its geographical borders as outsiders to whom much less is due than to insiders. By 'nationality', in contrast, I mean an identity constituted not by fixed characteristics but by understandings and commitments shared with co-nationals which are, in principle, open to collective revision; an identity that is not all-encompassing but that coexists with other identities people rely upon to give meaning to their lives; an identity focused on a geographical location and mediated through a historical tradition but not so parochial that it closes off cultural exchange; an identity that requires public expression but that recognises that other national identities have a similar requirement and does not depend upon political privileges denied to others.[7]

There is, it is true, no guarantee that nationality will not degenerate into nationalism. But the crucial point is that the two are different in kind, and nationality cannot be accused of possessing any impulse towards nationalism. Interestingly, this point is acknowledged by Kearney, whose own argument for a post-nationalist Ireland similarly distinguishes between the two and manages to find space for a national identity based on 'cultural memory, tradition, belonging'.[8] Whether the distinction would be accepted by either side in the dispute about nationalism represented in this volume is harder to decide. There are perhaps slight grounds for optimism given that O'Hagan makes a distinction between the kind of nationalism I have described above and what he refers to as a 'non-threatening' and 'everyday concept of nationalism'. In a sense, I am simply proposing that what I have called 'nationality' gives conceptual articulation to what he calls 'a feeling of specific belonging'. And although both Mansergh and McLaughlin freely appropriate the term 'nationalism' what they mean by it may be closer to my notion of nationality than to my account of nationalism. At the very least, the possibility of bridging differences between pro-nationalist and anti-nationalist republicans on this point is worth flagging up.

However that may be, the important question in this context is whether affections associated with nationality are reconcilable with the universal dimension of the United Irishmen's republicanism. I have little doubt that, in principle, they are. It is the very different affections associated with nationalism that cramp commitment to global concerns of justice and right, and that try to minimise the impact of such concerns in local situations. The fight, then, is in my view wrongly described as one between republicanism's universal dimension and national affections. It is better depicted instead as one between those affections congenial to universalism and those not. The Canadian thinker and political activist Charles Taylor aptly makes a similar point in a different context:

> In most cases our choice is not whether or not people will respond to mobilization around a common identity – as against, say, being recruitable only for universal causes – but which of two or more possible identities will claim their allegiance. Some of these will be wider than others, some more open and hospitable to cosmopolitan solidarities. It is between these that the battle for civilised cosmopolitanism must frequently be fought, and not in an impossible (and if successful, self-defeating) attempt to set aside all such patriotic identities ...we have no choice but to be cosmopolitans and patriots; which means to fight for the kind of patriotism which is open to universal solidarities against other, more closed kinds.[9]

My distinction between nationalism and nationality may also prove fruitful when addressing the other type of objection to any association between republicanism and nationalism, namely that such an association is pointless since current political realities indicate that nationalism has outlived its usefulness. This objection is typically tied to the claim that the nation-state is increasingly becoming an unhelpful political category. Kearney, for instance, contends that the

> ...nation-state has...become too large *and* too small as a model of contemporary Irish identity. Too large for the growing need of regional, participatory democracy; and too small for the increasing drift towards transnational exchange and power-sharing, at both British–Irish and European levels.[10]

And John Hume, leader of the SDLP, sees in the prospect of European regionalism the advent of a fresh republicanism that goes beyond traditional preoccupations of Irish nationalism:

> This is the real new republicanism, the development of processes which will allow people to preserve their culture, rights and dignity; to promote their well-being and have a means of controlling the forces which will affect their lives... this will

allow us better to fulfil our potential as a people; to contribute to our world; to rediscover ourselves in political relationships with those on the Continental mainland and to enjoy properly the inchoate European outlook and vision which was lost in our oppressive and obsessive relationship with Britain. It maintains the necessary synchrony between the scope of democratic and economic and technological circumstances. ... On this basis we can provide a social, regional and Irish dimension to our Europe.[11]

Gerry Adams, president of Sinn Féin, does not, however, 'agree with [Hume's] views on the outdatedness of the nation state, which [Sinn Féin regards] as the basis of democracy. Republicans do not believe that we are living in a post-nationalist world.'[12]

We are confronted here with competing interpretations of our political realities. With regard to these, there are grounds for maintaining that the vision of a Europe of the regions that the arguments of Kearney and Hume invoke is as yet more of an aspiration than an achieved result. It is still a little premature to write the obituary of the nation-state.[13] But that there is growing European cooperation and integration, and growing British–Irish cooperation too, cannot be denied. And Kearney and Hume are entirely right to see in these moves the increasing irrelevance of nationalism as an exclusive, parochial ideology. Of course, even if their vision were realised and we had regions rather than nation-states, these regions would still have to be held together by the sort of bonds or affections that nationality evokes. In other words, the type of outward-looking patriotism that Taylor refers to and the type of national identity that Kearney himself sees value in would remain indispensable. Finally here, although shifts towards an integrated Europe erode the significance of the border in Ireland, they do not – and regionalism itself does not – definitively resolve the question of partition.

The most significant move to address this question is mooted in the recent Belfast Agreement, to which all the republican parties represented in this book give their support. It proposes to change our current political realities in a way that challenges traditional Irish nationalism (and traditional unionism too, it should be added). Without going into details, proposals that have been put to and overwhelmingly passsed by the people of Ireland, in separate referenda North and South, include the establishment of a new Northern assembly based on principles of power-sharing rather than on those of majority rule, institutional recognition of the British–Irish composition of Northern Ireland, various forms of institutionalised cooperation between North and South, and a new set of relations between Ireland and Britain.

It may be that a republicanism tied to nationalism is ill equipped to make coherent sense of these proposals, except in a negative way. As dissident republicans of a staunchly nationalist disposition never tire of telling us, the proposals disturb fundamental components of traditional Irish nationalism. For example, the political unity of the Irish nation is reduced to an aspiration awaiting the consent of a majority of people in Northern Ireland. And this point is to be emphatically underlined by the removal of the Republic of Ireland's claim in its constitution to the territory of the whole island of Ireland. The old image of an independent and separatist Irish nation appears almost quaintly out of kilter with the agreement's recommendations of highly interdependent arrangements moving across North–South and East–West axes. The putative sovereignty of the Irish nation is sacrificed through formal recognition of British sovereignty in Northern Ireland, and even if certain of the anticipated North–South arrangements suggest an occasional pooling of sovereignty, this is small consolation on traditional nationalist terms. Furthermore, the cardinal principle of the Irish nation's right to self-determination is adjusted in a partitionist way that effectively sees it being replaced by a principle of co-determination, whereby the fate of Ireland is decided in separate referenda North and South.

Arguably, a republicanism tied to nationality can cope more easily with the proposed changes that cut traditional nationalism to the core. Nationality allows for changes in a nation's self-understandings, it is not hostile to other identities, and it is not intrinsically predisposed to political outcomes that involve their humiliation. Accordingly, it permits a more flexible approach to contemporary Irish politics, one capable of accepting that unity is an aspiration – and not a reality whose dawning can be hastened by a bit more armed struggle. And since it refers to an identity open to interchange it is not threatened by the interdependent relationships that subvert parochial certainties. Moreover, because it acknowledges the political entitlements of other identities, nationality is more prone to concede that, especially in the divided circumstances of the North, principles of sovereignty and self-determination are of concern to others besides Irish republicans and nationalists.

If nationality, rather than nationalism, facilitates a more welcoming acceptance of the agreement among Irish republicans, it does not necessarily entail any diminution of their desire for stronger links between North and South than those presently on offer. It does not demand that they stop aiming for a final end to partition. On the contrary, it simply circumscribes the sort of means they are prepared to employ in pursuit of their objectives, and it indicates the sort of relationships they are willing to build with those of a different national persuasion.

Now, whether all the republican parties who have indicated a willingness to make the agreement work would accept the foregoing analysis is no doubt another matter. I submit it here only as a possible way that republicans committed to a resolution of the national question may adjust to changing political circumstances without forfeiting their commitment. Granted these circumstances, it seems to me that the immediately crucial points for a republicanism associated with nationality are that Irishness is given public expression in the institutional life of the North, and that political power is brought under the control of citizens. There are now very real prospects of both these occurring.

## REPUBLICAN SOCIETY

These prospects bring to attention a priority mentioned by all contributors to this volume, namely that society – whether in Ireland, North or South, or in Britain – should be moulded in a more republican direction. I want to conclude by making a cursory observation about what this priority is broadly taken to mean, and by then asking three questions that bear on the idea of a republican society.

On the surface, all the contributors appear to have remarkably similar thoughts about how society might be shaped in a more republican way. All sectarian and other forms of discrimination – whether race- or gender-based – should be abandoned. Pluralism should be welcomed, individual and group rights should be respected, equality legislation should be implemented, and so on. These are worthy suggestions, but one hardly needs to be a republican to buy them. They would be found on almost any contemporary liberal agenda, for example. O'Hagan, however, certainly indicates that there is more to republicanism than liberalism when he claims that a republican society is necessarily one organised along socialist lines. But it is unclear how much agreement this claim would receive among the other contributors. On strictly party lines, it is a reasonable bet that Cook, Mansergh and Hanna would have difficulties with the type of socialist arrangements O'Hagan has in mind. It is perhaps a slightly more open question how far McLaughlin as well as Kilmurray and McWilliams would travel down the road of O'Hagan's socialism.

Now I do not doubt that republicanism does share much with liberalism and with socialism, but exploring how much is beyond my extremely brief purposes here. Instead I want to ask questions that prompt reflection on the possibility of there being a distinctively republican conception of society, one that cannot simply be explained in terms of another political philosophy regardless of how many overlapping emphases they share.

First, then, does republicanism entail commitment to a

particular political value? A clue that it does is implied in the point made by Kilmurray and McWilliams that a concept of active citizenship is at the core of civic republicanism. Expressed another way, this is to say that republicans recognise the intrinsic value of a self-rule by citizens that invokes a strong notion of political participation. This, then, becomes a primary political good for republicans in a way that it is not, say, for most liberals. Citizenship is primarily important for contemporary liberals inasmuch as it secures individuals' (and perhaps also groups') entitlements to equal rights and opportunities. Republicans typically think that this is a necessary but not a sufficient understanding of citizenship – an understanding that puts insufficient stress on the value of participation. On republican terms, citizen participation is so indispensable to the conduct of politics that society should be structured to ensure its effective possibility.

An obvious second question is how widely participation should be understood. As I have argued at greater length elsewhere, given the conditions of the contemporary West it entails not just involvement in the life of the state and the formal apparatuses of political parties and bureaucracies, but also involvement in the life of civil society.[14] The trick is to integrate these spheres of activity, so that political power is not exercised at a remove from citizens' lives and so that the energies of civic activists are not politically ineffectual. This is particularly important in Northern Ireland, where a thriving community and voluntary sector has operated relatively independently of the major political parties, who have themselves been denied access to any meaningful power. The possibility of a devolved assembly in Northern Ireland promises to satisfy the needs of the parties, and the agreement's suggested introduction of a consultative civic forum to supplement the assembly gives hope of institutional recognition of the importance of civil society. Taken together, assembly and forum offer rare opportunities for a fruitful interrelationship between political and civic concerns in a manner that encourages meaningful citizen participation in various areas of social and political life.

A third question asks what sort of conditions are required to promote such participation and to counteract political alienation and apathy among citizens. This is an unavoidable question if participation in self-government is regarded as a primary political good, and if it is understood to involve at its core deliberating with fellow citizens. A clear condition of effective participation or deliberation is that citizens possess a knowledge of public affairs, a condition that minimally requires educational initiatives to provide a basic grounding in politics and relevant disciplines. Another condition of capital importance is that citizens have a lively sense of belonging to their society, crucial to which is an identification with their public institutions. In the context of Northern Ireland, and as the Belfast Agreement appreciates, this is only possible through a recognition of both British and Irish identities in institutional life. Without such dual recognition the alienation of a large number of citizens is inevitable. And any society whose basic institutions cannot command widespread citizen allegiance is a society threatening to atrophy. Those political actors who refuse to support the agreement because they are holding out for exclusively British or Irish solutions to problems in the North have, among other things, little understanding of an important facet of republican politics. Admittedly, only those seeking a purely Irish solution are likely to be irked by such a claim.

Other conditions relevant to the promotion of effective political participation include that citizens should have a concern for the whole political community and not just one set of interests, and that they should develop a moral bond with the entire community whose fate is at stake in their deliberations. These conditions suggest, in short, that it is not enough for citizens simply to advocate the concerns of their particular national identities; the sustainability of institutions and practices conducive to participation also requires citizens to embrace more expansive self-understandings which accommodate the possibility of a shared civic identity. In the old language of a civic republicanism whose roots can be traced to Aristotle, this is to say that political participation involves the cultivation of civic virtues among citizens. As the North American political philosopher Michael Sandel puts it, 'republican politics cannot be neutral toward the values and ends its citizens espouse'; rather, what is required is 'a formative politics, a politics that cultivates in citizens the qualities of character self-government requires'.[15] The point here is that the all-too-familiar poses in northern politics, of defending one's corner and of trying only to win benefits for one's tribe, betray seriously impoverished understandings of the qualities required for self-government.

Talk of the cultivation of such qualities only makes sense, of course, if another condition is attended to, namely the creation of social and economic circumstances conducive to citizen participation. A society that treats the self-government of citizens as a primary good is one that refuses to allow any of its citizens to fall below a certain economic threshold; it is one that provides opportunities for citizens' flourishing by implementing across the board of social and economic life – from employment to wages, from health care to pensions, from education to social benefits – policies that are designed to instil in them a sense of dignity. The possession of such dignity is a necessary prerequisite of constructive political engagement.

The fleeting answers I have sketched to questions concerning the possibility of developing a distinctively republican conception of society may not, of course, be shared by the other contributors to this volume. My hunch is that opinions would vary, and that certain of my suggestions would appear more palatable than others. But since in some fashion or another all the following essays address the idea of a republican society, it is entirely appropriate to enquire what such an idea might mean. My central claim is that if, as my earlier analysis submits, it is mistaken to regard republicanism as a species of nationalism, it is similarly mistaken to regard it as a species of either liberalism or socialism. To claim this is no doubt to invite controversy. But at least it has the virtue of reiterating one of the major messages of this book: the republican ideal admits of various interpretations and prompts all sorts of different lines of enquiry. It is an ideal that 200 years on from the events of 1798 retains its vitality and its capacity to capture a range of political imaginations.

## NOTES

1. Charles Spinosa, Fernando Flores, and Hubert Dreyfus, 'Disclosing New Worlds: Entrepreneurship, Democratic Action, and the Cultivation of Solidarity', *Inquiry*, vol. 38 (June 1995), p. 25.
2. Jürgen Habermas, 'Citizenship and National Identity: Some Reflections on the Future of Europe', *Praxis International*, vol. 12, no. 1 (1992), p. 3.
3. Richard Kearney, *Postnationalist Ireland: Politics, Culture, Philosophy* (London: Routledge, 1997), p. 29.
4. *Ibid.*, p. 30.
5. Michael Walzer, 'Spheres of Affection', *Boston Review*, vol. 19 (1994), p. 25.
6. Martha Nussbaum, 'Patriotism and Cosmopolitanism', *Boston Review*, vol. 19 (1994), p. 3.
7. I am indebted for these thoughts on nationality to David Miller, *On Nationality* (Oxford: Oxford University Press, 1995), pp. 17–48.
8. Kearney, *Postnationalist Ireland*, p. 59.
9. Charles Taylor, 'Why Democracy Needs Patriotism', *Boston Review*, vol. 19 (1994), p. 26.
10. Kearney, *Postnationalist Ireland*, p. 20.
11. John Hume quoted in *ibid.*, p. 37.
12. Gerry Adams, *Selected Writings* (Dingle: Brandon Books, 1997), p. 325.
13. See Dennis Kennedy, 'The European Union and the Northern Ireland Question', in Brian Barton and Patrick Roche (eds.), *The Northern Ireland Question: Policies and Perspectives* (Aldershot: Avebury, 1994).
14. Norman Porter, *Rethinking Unionism: An Alternative Vision for Northern Ireland* (Belfast: Blackstaff Press, 1996), pp. 201–2.
15. Michael Sandel, *Democracy's Discontent: America in Search of a Public Philosophy* (Cambridge, Mass.: Harvard University Press, 1996), p. 6.

# 2

# The Republican Ideal Regained

## MARTIN MANSERGH

THE LEGACY OF 1916: LEGITIMACY AND PRAGMATISM

The 1916 Proclamation and rising have remained the central locus of Irish republicanism. Surprisingly, in his writings prior to the Easter Rising, Pádraig Pearse laid relatively little emphasis on republicanism *per se*. What mattered to him was the spirit of nationality and the separatist ideal, and it was against that standard that he measured Tone, Davis, Lalor and Mitchel, and even Parnell.[1]

Much like the American Declaration of Independence of 1776, the 1916 Proclamation was the founding charter of a new state. The ostensible motive of the rising was to stage a large military demonstration to renew the flame of Irish nationality. In the opinion of the dissident wing of the Irish Volunteers, that flame was in danger of being extinguished through a Redmondite identification with the British Empire in its struggle to save (other) small nations. Pearse himself was more ambitious, and if he had illusions about the military potential of the rising, which had no more than demonstration value in purely military terms, these seem to have been combined with an uncannily accurate foresight of its immense psychological impact, even in the event of failure. In his poem 'The Fool', Pearse wrote prophetically of his 'attempting impossible things':

> 'O wise men, riddle me this: what if the dream come true?
> What if the dream come true? and if millions unborn shall dwell
> In the house that I shaped in my heart, the noble house of my thought?[2]

The Proclamation invoked God and the dead generations and Ireland's old tradition of nationhood, and made reference to the support of exiles in America and gallant allies in Europe. The latter reference to a largely indifferent Germany at war was a mistake, contrary to the original spirit of neutrality; it fed British phobias about Britain's 'selfish strategic interest', and put the insurgents in the General Post Office (GPO) in Dublin on the opposite side of those Irishmen on the Western Front, whether from the unionist or the constitutional nationalist tradition. There was nothing particularly gallant about the Kaiser's Germany compared to the other countries involved in the slaughter of the trenches, nor after 1914 did it provide any effective help, whilst earlier Germany had been equally sympathetic to Carson, and in fact sold more guns for illegal importation to the Ulster Volunteer Force (UVF) than to the Irish Volunteers. De Valera indicated a fundamental change of policy in the United States in 1920 in the middle of the War of Independence when, much to the annoyance of such Irish-American supporters as John Devoy, he expressed a willingness to accept a Monroe Doctrine for Ireland, namely that it would not allow itself to be used as a base from which a foreign power could attack Britain. Efforts have been made to denigrate the ideals of the rising, exploiting a passing reference in the memoirs of Desmond FitzGerald to discussion amongst those occupying the GPO about the possible interest of a Hohenzollern prince in the throne of Ireland. It was speculative banter about possible German designs not Irish desires, of the type that Wolfe Tone engaged in about French intentions in the Paris of the 1790s. Weighed against the solemnity of the Proclamation, this piece of distraction has been invested with a ludicrously exaggerated importance by some historians or commentators mostly unsympathetic either to the 1916 rising or to the republican tradition.[3]

An absolute claim was made in the Proclamation about the right of the people of Ireland to the ownership of Ireland and to sovereignty. No rights had been established by long usurpation, it stated; in other words, there had been no consent to conquest in its many different guises. The Republic guaranteed religious and civil liberty, equal rights and equal opportunities to all its citizens, 'cherishing all the children of the nation equally'. The Proclamation did not express an ethos of majoritarian rule in religious terms, and as my late father Nicholas Mansergh wrote in his preface to the third edition of *The Irish Question*, 'there was no easy going back on that'.[4] The Republic promised the establishment, as soon as arms had brought the opportune moment, of democratic government elected by universal suffrage of men and women. Pearse had written of 1798 in 'The Spiritual Nation': 'If we accept the definition of Irish freedom as "the Rights of Man in Ireland" we shall find it difficult to imagine an apostle of Irish freedom who is not a democrat.'[5] While there is no doubt that the 1916 leaders envisaged a fully democratic government, the temporary arrogation of political authority by a small, unrepresentative conspiratorial minority, even if given a large measure of *ex post facto* justification and democratic sanction in the 1918 general election, inevitably caused significant unease, both then and subsequently. The signatories to the Proclamation finally prayed that no one would dishonour the cause of the Irish Republic by inhumanity or rapine. It was the last time the hopeless chivalry of open warfare (which following 1798 had been rejected as a viable option by most Irish political and Church leaders) would be displayed on Irish soil.

The key idea in the Proclamation was a claim to self-determination, as it would soon be known, by the people of Ireland, a claim deriving its force from the historic Irish nation defeated in the seventeenth century. The question of private property ownership was left open, Pearse having a more pragmatic view on this than Connolly. There was to be tolerance and inclusion for minorities, and equality of opportunity, as well as political equality, for men and women. The phrase 'cherishing all the children of the nation equally' also had potentially a strong social message. Seán Lemass later said: 'Those who fought in the Rising visualised freedom... not as an end in itself, but as an opportunity of wiping out the squalor, decay, depression and ignorance which external rule had signified in Ireland.'[6] Following the executions of leaders of the rising, there was an irreversible sea-change in public opinion in favour of the ideals of those who had been shot, and, to paraphrase Yeats, a terrible beauty was born.[7]

Throughout the whole period from the scheme for devolution in 1905 to the Treaty debate, there was always to be an inverse interrelationship, at least in the short to medium term, between unity among the Irish people and sovereignty. If Irish men and women of all traditions had been able to work together, as the Independent Orange Order desired in the Magheramorne Manifesto of 1905, a modest form of devolution or a restricted form of Home Rule would have sufficed at least for the time being as a starting and as a rallying point. But if the reward for moderation and self-denial on the part of the nationalist majority was still adamant unionist resistance to any form of self-government, however limited, at least so far as the six counties were concerned, then what was the point of compromising so heavily on sovereignty? Not unfairly, Carson received some of the blame for the 1916 rising. The failure of the Irish Convention of 1917–18 to reach some all-Ireland compromise played heavily into the hands of Sinn Féin. The problem with the Treaty signed in 1921 was that it did not give the Irish people clear satisfaction either on their preferred constitutional status as a sovereign republic or on unity. Sir Alfred Cope, the chief British civil servant in Dublin, realised that that was neither viable nor tenable, as the Treaty negotiations were about to begin, but he was ignored.[8]

The 1916 Proclamation was reinforced by the 1919 Declaration of Independence, by the 1919 Democratic Programme of the first Dáil, and by the sacrifices of the War of Independence. However, neither of the 1919 documents, one of which explicitly equated a free Ireland with a Gaelic Ireland (and to all intents and purposes a Catholic one), and the other which put forward a strong social programme, acquired the same status subsequently as the 1916 Proclamation. While some pragmatism was shown on the question of partition, to the extent of renouncing coercion against the unionist national minority in their strongholds, renunciation of the declared Republic as well, as the price of virtual political independence, was too much for some to swallow.

Liam Lynch, leader of the republican forces during the civil war, stated after the signing of the Treaty: 'We have declared for a Republic, and will not live under any other law'.[9] During the Dáil debates on the Treaty, Mary MacSwiney spoke of the Republic almost as if it were a Platonic ideal:

> It was a minority that fought in 1916; it is always a minority that saves the soul of a nation in its hour of need. This fight of ours has been essentially a spiritual fight, a fight of a small people struggling for a spiritual ideal against a mighty rapacious and material Empire. It is those who stand for the spiritual and the ideal that stand true and unflinching.[10]

De Valera, unlike some of the more intransigent anti-Treatyites who wanted an isolated republic, was prepared to contemplate Ireland's external association as a republic with the British Commonwealth (a solution that would have spared incalculable grief and economic damage), as well as guarantees of Britain's essential strategic interests, which got him into a lot of trouble with some leading Irish-Americans. Collins took the pragmatic view that it was the evacuation of the British army that counted, and that this would create the freedom to achieve freedom. With the British, and especially Churchill and his advisers, determined to scotch any compromise with the Republic that might conflict with the dominion status imposed in the Treaty, an essentially hopeless and deeply demoralising civil war ensued, fought with much reluctance on both sides most of the time. Even though militarily defeated in 1923, and accepting the principle of decision by majority voting as necessary for order and unity in national action, republicans did not accept the political legitimacy of the Irish Free State as originally constituted.

For some time, the fiction that the second Dáil remained in session and that its remaining members constituted the actual 'Government of the Republic' was maintained by republicans, while the Free State institutions were being steadily consolidated. There was a danger of marginalisation and increasing irrelevance. By early 1926, Lemass was exasperated with debating 'abstruse points about a *de jure* this and a *de facto* that'.[11] When Sinn Féin declined by a narrow majority to have anything to do with participation in either the Dáil or Stormont, even if the oath of allegiance to the crown were removed, de Valera and many of his followers left Sinn Féin and formed a new republican party, Fianna Fáil, in May 1926. Most of the republican mainstream were brought into Fianna Fáil, including many of the relatives of the 1916 leaders, such as Pádraig Pearse's mother and sister, Mrs Tom Clarke (who later parted company) and, before she died in 1927, Countess Markievicz.

While the three main political forces of the new state, Fianna Fáil, Fine Gael and Labour, were the principal heirs of 1916, Fianna Fáil was to all intents and purposes the successor of the republican side in the civil war. Michael Collins and his close followers were equally republican, albeit more pragmatic about means. The rapid political success of Fianna Fáil demonstrated that allied to parliamentary participation and a dynamic economic and social policy the Irish people had a much greater empathy with the political ideals of republicanism than with any new or continued armed insurrection. In the 1930s, the Treaty was largely dismantled by de Valera and Fianna Fáil, and by 1937 Ireland chose a president and had to all intents and purposes a new republican constitution, to which the British government elected to turn a blind eye. The main purpose of articles 2 and 3 of the constitution was to signify the continued withholding of consent to partition, in repudiation of the acceptance of the border in the 1925 Boundary Agreement negotiated by the Free State government of W.T. Cosgrave.

The Sinn Féin residue, however, claimed over decades to retain for themselves the legitimacy of the 'lost republican ideal', and the last survivor of the second Dáil, General Thomas Maguire, purported to hand on the torch not just with others in 1938 to the IRA, but ultimately to Republican Sinn Féin, which had itself split away in 1986 from the modern republican movement, itself the product of an earlier split, in 1969.[12] It was always possible to trace a convoluted legitimist thread equivalent to an unbroken apostolic succession. Under pressure to justify itself, the modern republican movement itself has often claimed to derive its legitimacy from the 1918 general election. May 1926, like December 1921 and a number of subsequent dates, was one of the many forks in the road for Irish republicanism. The main body of republicans in the South since 1926 is identified with Fianna Fáil, while in the North Sinn Féin has the support currently of one-sixth of the electorate, or over 40 per cent of the nationalist vote. Some representatives of other parties also identify themselves as republican or express their ideals in republican language.

REPUBLICANISM: A HISTORICAL AND INTERNATIONAL PERSPECTIVE

Whilst warring kings existed back into the mists of time and mythology, monarchy represented a fall from the ideal, whether one examines the classical world or the Bible. The Greek city-state, which was the earliest form of democracy (complete with slaves), was a little republic. Self-governing cities, as small states that were republics, were a feature of the political organisation of Europe up to the French Revolution, a few, like Switzerland, surviving into the modern age.

The essence of Plato's ideal republic was justice: that 'no... government provides for its own benefit, but... it provides and prescribes what is for the benefit of the subject, seeking the advantage of him who is weaker, not the advantage of the stronger'.[13] A degree of egalitarianism, even if confined to a limited political elite, underlay the refusal to confer power permanently on one individual or family, who would be in a position to suspend or subvert the law. The Roman republic for much of its existence combined aristocratic rule with populist elements. Cicero's ideal political arrangement was one 'where government was in the control of the State's *principes*, but in a free society that accepted and supported their ascendancy'.[14] Shakespeare's Julius Caesar limply pushes away the imperial crown, while the conspirators complain that he bestrides the world like a Colossus and that it is their fault if they are underlings. The decline and fall of the Roman empire began in the corruption of the post-Augustan era.

As Thomas Paine pointed out in his influential and devastating pamphlet for the American colonists in revolt in 1776, *Common Sense*, the God of the old Testament (I Samuel 8) strongly disapproved of kings. Paine played down, however, the fact that the Israelites wanted to replace the theocratic government of the prophets with a civil and military royal government as it existed elsewhere. Addressing a Protestant audience, some of it fundamentalist in character, Paine stated that the will of the Almighty, as declared by Gideon and the prophet Samuel, expressly disapproved of government by kings; he described monarchy as 'the Popery of Government'. He argued that 'the state of a king shuts him from the world, yet the business of a king requires him to know it thoroughly', and that no power 'which needs checking' can be from God. Hereditary right was 'a degradation and lessening of ourselves', as well as 'an insult and an imposition on posterity'. 'For all men being originally equals, no one by birth could have a right to set up his own family in perpetual preference to all others for ever.'[15] Nor did hereditary kingship prevent civil war and rebellion, as English (and indeed French) history showed. Elizabeth I set a fatal precedent for Charles I by beheading Mary, Queen of Scots, and Charles's example in turn impinged upon Louis XVI and Tsar Nicholas II and their families.

In a contemporary Irish context, it is a complete reversal of alliances that in the main the Presbyterians with their democratic and anti-hierarchical form of church government should be loyalist, while republicans in the main are Catholic. In the late seventeenth and the eighteenth centuries, the loyalty of Ulster Presbyterians was deeply suspect to the authorities. James II in a memorandum of advice warned his son that the New English, the Protestants, were generally republicans, whereas he praised the great loyalty the native Catholics had shown.[16] Swift regarded Dissenters with an equally jaundiced eye. It is notable that the Americans of Ulster Presbyterian stock were prominent in the War of Independence, whereas the Scottish Highlanders who had been Jacobite were generally loyalist. Irish Catholics on the other hand wanted a Stuart king in the Catholic interest, and – as Piaras Beáslaí pointed out with some justice in the Treaty debate – neither the Catholic Confederates of the 1640s nor the spokesmen for the Hidden Ireland of the eighteenth century were republican.[17]

The French Revolution produced the novelty of republicanism in a hitherto Catholic country. Wolfe Tone wrote:

> When I contrast the National Assembly of Frenchmen and Catholics with other great Bodies, which I could name, I confess I feel I have little propensity to boast that I have the honour to be an Irishman and a Protestant.[18]

What answer could be made to the Catholics of Ireland if they were to demand their full civil rights, he wondered. He further asked 'if we are still illiberal and blind bigots, who deny that civil liberty can exist out of the pale of Protestantism?' That type of self-critical challenge was and is a relatively rare phenomenon in the Irish Protestant tradition.

The first republicans in Ireland were Cromwellians. The statue of Cromwell outside the Palace of Westminster underscores to this day the supremacy of parliament *vis-à-vis* the monarch. The Stuart restoration was accepted in Ireland on the basis that with the exception of the holdings of a few regicides the Cromwellian land settlement was to be maintained. England confirmed its latent (by now aristocratic) republicanism when it dethroned James II and his descendants in 1688, and again in 1714 when it put the Elector of Hanover on the throne in preference to another Stuart.

Dutch William was the great-grandson of William the Silent, who had thrown off Spanish absolutism and religious intolerance, and who strove unsuccessfully to create a united and independent Dutch republic that would show tolerance to Protestant, Catholic and Dissenter. (William the Silent had been all three, and as a result would have been ineligible to be a member of the Orange Order!) The first William of Orange was one of the great defenders of civil and religious liberty, and repeatedly refused the Dutch crown.[19]

The Glorious Revolution, while producing oligarchy and Protestant Ascendancy in the eighteenth century, nevertheless helped to inspire through the ideas of its philosopher John Locke the American and French revolutions. It was John Locke who destroyed the intellectual foundations of a paternalistic absolute monarchy based on conquest, in favour of government being only legitimate if based on consent, which had to be won.[20]

The *philosophes* in eighteenth century France took Locke a stage further. Montesquieu, who belonged to the magistrate caste, presented republics as an equally valid form of government, in either their aristocratic or democratic form, to monarchies and despotisms.[21] Rousseau in his *Du contrat social* wrote that 'man was born free, and is everywhere in chains'. If there were a people made up of gods, they would govern themselves democratically. He claimed that in *The Prince* Machiavelli gave great lessons to peoples, while purporting to counsel kings, and that it was the bible of republicans. (De Valera would probably have agreed!)[22]

Francis Hutcheson, Ireland's greatest political philosopher, who taught in Dublin and Glasgow in the early eighteenth century, and who was one of the leading ornaments of the Scottish Enlightenment, believed strongly in accountable government and the people's right to change their rulers. He believed the ideal state was a small republic where rulers and ruled stayed close to each other.[23]

The United States presents the model of a successfully established republic founded on classical principles. The Declaration of Independence of 1776, mainly drafted by Thomas Jefferson, stated with succinct eloquence: 'We hold these truths to be self-evident, that all men are created equal, that they are endowed by their Creator with certain inalienable rights, that among these are life, liberty, and the pursuit of happiness.' The American Republic was established with a constitution containing an elaborate separation of powers, which sought to protect minorities from the much-feared tyranny of the majority. The presidency was intended to be an austere institution, free of monarchical despotism or corruption. Eighty-seven years after the Declaration of Independence, in his famous Gettysburg Address of 1863 in the midst of a bloody civil war, President Abraham Lincoln reaffirmed the ideas of the founding fathers and 'of a new nation, conceived in liberty, and dedicated to the proposition that all men are created equal', renewing the resolve 'that this nation, under God, shall have a new birth of freedom; and that government of the people, by the people and for the people, shall not perish from the earth'.

With all its defects and all its problems, the United States is the most powerful country on earth, not just because of its size or population, but because of the moral quality and adaptability of its principles of government over a long, two-hundred-year period, unmatched by any other country.

The French Revolution began in an atmosphere of even greater idealism, as it destroyed such symbols of oppression as the Bastille, and dismantled the hierarchy, monopolies and feudal residues of the *ancien régime*. The Declaration of the Rights of Man and of the Citizen was the manifesto of the French Revolution. While paying lip service at first to constitutional monarchy, its spirit was already republican, one and indivisible. Article 3 of the declaration states that 'the principle of all sovereignty resides essentially in the nation' (in contrast to the monarch).[24] The declaration guaranteed the right to democratic participation in law-making, careers open to talent, the rule of law and the presumption of innocence, religious tolerance subject to public order, liberty of the press, taxation according to ability to pay, and public accountability. Unfortunately, the excesses of the Terror, followed by a period of corruption under the Directory, discredited the memory of the First Republic, which soon had to struggle against the more glamorous imperial vision of Napoleon, the more conservative and reactionary throne and altar of the Bourbon Restoration, and the experiment of bourgeois monarchy under the citizen king Louis-Philippe; even the Second Republic succeeded to its *ersatz* form under Louis-Napoleon.

Lazare Hoche, one of the leading generals of the French Republic, a rival to Bonaparte and commander of the abortive Bantry Bay expedition of 1796, had spent a spell in prison during the Terror before subsequently pacifying the Catholic and royalist Vendée. He told Wolfe Tone:

> ... great mischief has been done to the principles of liberty, and additional difficulties thrown in the way of the French Revolution, by the quantity of the blood spilled. [For] when you guillotine a man, you get rid of an individual, it is true, but then you make all his friends and family enemies for ever to the Government.[25]

Hoche died young, but he left behind a number of valuable republican maxims:

> Pity those who do not know how to love the people despite their faults and serve them despite their ingratitude.
>
> Reputations fall, and the people remain standing.
>
> One cannot make the republic loved by devastating property and by carrying sword and flame among the inhabitants.
>
> In the soul of republicans there are sentiments of justice and humanity and the greatest horror for bloodthirsty monsters.
>
> True republicans do not commit crimes.
>
> I have told the Directory twenty times, if it does not allow religious tolerance, it must give up any hope of peace in this country [the Vendée].[26]

Hoche's monument in his native Versailles states that he 'died too soon for France'. In an implied criticism of Napoleon, it added, 'If he had lived, his ever-increasing reputation would never have cost anything to the freedom of his country.'

If the French Revolution failed to accredit fully republicanism in the modern world, it inflicted serious, indeed near-terminal, damage on monarchy as a guarantor of order and stability. Jefferson, who had been US ambassador to Versailles, was scathing:

> Louis XVI was a fool, of my own knowledge, and in despite of the answers made for him at his trial. The King of Spain was a fool, and of Naples the same. They passed their lives in hunting and despatched two couriers a week, one thousand miles, to let each other know what game they had killed the preceding days... All these were Bourbons. The King of Prussia, successor to the great Frederick, was a mere hog in body as well as in mind. Gustavus of Sweden, and Joseph of Austria, were really crazy, and George of England, you know, was in a straight waistcoat. There remained then none but old Catherine, who had been too lately picked up to have lost her common sense. In this state Bonaparte found Europe: and it was this state of its rulers which lost it with scarce a struggle... And so endeth the book of kings, from all of whom the Lord deliver us.[27]

Many of those who subsequently married into royal families, such as Elisabeth (Sissy), who married the Emperor Franz Josef of Austria, or indeed Diana, Princess of Wales, whose life also ended prematurely and tragically, had or developed serious doubts about the long-term viability of the entire institution of monarchy. The Empresss Elisabeth wrote in her diary in 1884: 'The fact is, no one believes in kings any more, and I do not know if they even believe in themselves.' Her friend the queen of Romania wrote around the same time:

> I must sympathise with the social democrats, particularly given the inactivity and corruption of the great; these people only want what nature provides: equality. The republican state form is the only rational one; I can never understand the foolish people, how they still tolerate us.[28]

Present-day monarchs, reduced to being symbolic heads of state, depend entirely for their existence on continuing popular support, with no real power to command obedience. But whilst most European monarchies have pared down their courts to an almost bourgeois minimum, the survival of aristocracies and anachronistic-sounding honours encourages flummery and sycophancy. In Britain, the House of Lords permits the scions of families that were once hereditary oppressors of Ireland to dabble still in troubled waters, if they choose.

Nevertheless, attachment to ancient instituions – and they can have a long after-life, even when they have been initially demolished – remains strong, and Burke undoubtedly had a case, even if his sentimental devotion to the memory of the young Marie-Antoinette and the chivalry of the French nobility (shown much more convincingly in a massive tableau under the cupola on Capitol Hill alongside Washington receiving the surrender of Cornwallis at Yorktown) blinded him to the fact that the sect of economists had also grown up at Versailles around Louis xv's physician, Dr Quesnay.[29] Faith or loyalty replaces reason.

Yet the Enlightenment philosopher Immanuel Kant in his essay 'On Perpetual Peace' had a serious point when he claimed that a republican constitution and a European confederation of free states had the best chance of guaranteeing peace. This would prevent dynastic wars against the interests of the people, and the perceived *raisons d'état* that had led to three partitions of Poland, to the eternal infamy of the so-called enlightened despots, and to the discredit of the age of reason. The critique of despots would equally apply to military régimes and dictatorships of all kinds. Kant in certain respects prefigured the European Union.[30]

Despite 1848, republicanism was not finally established across Europe as the dominant form of government until the collapse of the Central European empires at the end of the First World War. In the case of Russia, the successor state was a union of a radical socialist republics, confederal in name only, based on the ideology of Marx and Lenin, and in its ruthlessness harking back to the Jacobins, though far exceeding them in brutality because more discreet. But the equation of socialism with republicanism, which had some attractions for a limited few in Ireland as well, did not either in the short or the long term succeed. In Western Europe, the undefeated victorious British did not believe the right to national self-determination proclaimed by US President Wilson should apply to Ireland.

Republicanism was a force, too, on other continents. In Latin America in the early nineteenth century, Bernardo O'Higgins, the hero of Chilean independence and of Irish parentage, was a republican in his actions.

> He abolished the numerous titles of nobility, describing them as hieroglyphics which had no place in a free nation. He established a Legion of Merit on French lines. He introduced toleration for dissenters, established primary schools, and the liberty of the press, and planned to divide entailed estates, at which point he succumbed to forceful vested interests.[31]

The European revolutions of 1848 proceeded in a similar spirit. French republicanism post-1870 was based on a vigorous separation of church and state.

## IRISH REPUBLICANISM FROM THE 1790s

Irish republicanism in the 1790s was American, French and secular in inspiration. It was primarily a means of realising and effecting complete separation from Britain. Its intended leader, Lord Edward FitzGerald, was married to Pamela, the presumed daughter of Philippe-Egalité, duke of Orléans, who in the National Assembly had voted for his cousin Louis XVI's death. The leaders of the United Irishmen in 1798 were democrats, who had been turned by repression into hardened revolutionaries. They were in passionate opposition to an oppressive government and a corrupt monopolistic ascendancy, seeking equal civil and religious liberty for all. Their anti-Orange propaganda disastrously backfired, and the perception was assiduously encouraged by their enemies of a Catholic rising in Wexford followed by sectarian massacre and retaliation, reawakening fears of 1641 and 1689, and this was enough to alienate a sufficient part of an enlightened northern opinion.

1848 gave a new impetus to Irish republicanism, swaying the more radical supporters of Young Ireland such as John Mitchel. It provided us with a national flag based on the prevalent notion that Orange and Green could be brought together. Two decades later, the Fenians included both separatists and republicans, but their hope that Britain would become embroiled in the American Civil War was never realised. Indeed, Irish exiles living in the United States found themselves on opposite sides in that war, green against green, and some never wanted to put themselves in that position again. Much of the Fenians' energy was spent warding off the Church, but they also noted that their Protestant support had dwindled away the further 1782 receded in time. The Fenian torch was picked up by Pearse at the grave of O'Donovan Rossa in 1915. It is ironic that Michael Collins, as head of the Irish Republican Brotherhood (IRB) from 1919 was president of the Irish Republic 'virtually established' in 1867, whilst Eamon de Valera was President of the Irish Republic proclaimed anew in 1919, which also remained to be fully established and recognised, adding a pointed dimension to their later rivalry.

De Valera, even or especially in 1921–22, as well as in subsequent years, sought to establish a constitutional republicanism. Where he failed in the early 1920s, he succeeded in the 1930s. In 1937 he deliberately stopped short of crossing every *t* and dotting every *i*, because he wanted to leave some bridge open to the unionists. In 1948, Costello sought to trump him by declaring a republic and leaving the British Commonwealth, thus ending any vestige of ambiguity about the status of the new state; the formal declaration of the Republic took place in 1949.

The British retaliated by removing any vestige of ambiguity about their guarantee to the unionists. The real had been proclaimed the ideal, rather than the other way round, and a vigorous anti-partition campaign was begun to try to close the wide gap between the two. That campaign's rhetoric, its failure and its abandonment may have had some contributing influence on the starting up of the IRA's border campaign of 1956–62. Similarly, the assertive character of the commemoration of the fiftieth anniversary of the Easter Rising in 1966 may have unintentionally cut across the spirit of North–South détente and rapprochement under Lemass and O'Neill.

The subsequent civil rights movement, after some major early achievements, was overtaken by a reversion to armed struggle and to the guerrilla tactics of the war of independence. But the situations were not comparable. The modern IRA only ever represented a minority section of one community in the North, not a majority even of nationalists. The British state was able to assimilate it to international terrorism, which all Western states were committed to combat, and unionists could plausibly present their community and their identity as under threat. Now, at the end of nearly thirty years, whatever the other changes that may have resulted from the conflict, it is difficult to maintain that a united Ireland is any closer to achievement. Republicanism had in practice even before the conflict been moving steadily further away from the ideal of uniting Protestant, Catholic and Dissenter under the common name of Irishman. Seán Lemass was aware of this when he said in 1964 that it would be good if in educational establishments, and in University College Dublin in particular, Wolfe Tone's concept of the Irish nation was better understood and respected.[32]

The notion of the revolutionary elite, derived from Pearse and the Fenians and partly from international example, lost credibility when, outside of certain strongholds, the people persistently refused to follow, and when the world of Lenin collapsed in 1989–90 all over Europe. After a conflict, mainly in Northern Ireland, that had resulted in well over three thousand deaths but brought the desired result no closer, a new project was badly needed.

DE VALERA REPUBLICANISM AND ITS SUBSEQUENT EVOLUTION

For close on half a century, Eamon de Valera represented the mainstream republican tradition North and South. In his roles as president both of Sinn Féin from 1917 to 1921 and of the Irish Republic and later from 1932 as taoiseach, he was the principal architect of an Irish nation-state, to the consolidation of which he gave the main priority. Like Konrad Adenauer in a partitioned Germany, de Valera was in the circumstances of his time a state builder rather than the unifier of a nation. One would not interfere with the other, as his solution envisaged the same degree of autonomy for the six counties under Irish sovereignty as Northern Ireland enjoyed under the Government of Ireland Act 1920, provided discrimination was banished. Sometimes misleadingly referred to as a federal solution, it was in fact devolved government within a unitary state (or, at most, a quasi-federal state).

De Valera was the first to accept in his correspondence with Lloyd George that 'we do not envisage the use of force', partly because he wanted Lloyd George on the same principle to renounce coercion for good against the rest of Ireland and allow it the status it had chosen, of a republic, if necessary externally associated with the Commonwealth. Despite this, physical coercion was attempted by Collins and Mulcahy, in collusion with some of the Irregulars in 1922, with arguably disastrous and counterproductive results in terms of what we would nowadays call 'ethnic cleansing' and reinforcement of the unionist siege mentality. After that experience, radicals believed that the only way forward was via republican socialism, emphasising working-class solidarity and common interests across the divide. The theory was put to the test in Belfast in the mid-1930s, when Orangeism easily triumphed over socialism.

The situation post-1921 was complicated by the fact that the six-county area contained two counties and indeed other districts where nationalists were in a clear majority, until gerrymandering could be brought into play to obscure this fact. The British finesse over the Boundary Commission, including the old Lloyd George trick of encouraging opposing parties to believe opposite things, and the drastic weakening of the Irish negotiating position as a consequence of the civil war, allowed unionists to get away with their tactics, but with no good long-term results.

The 1925 Boundary Agreement, without being explicit, appeared to confirm the boundary *de jure*, this was vigorously repudiated by de Valera, though the constitution enacted in 1937 did not challenge the *de facto* position. De Valera was well aware of discrimination and gerrymandering, but nevertheless put the primary emphasis on the constitutional issue and on Britain's role in resolving it, as opposed to any direct and in all probability at that time fruitless negotiation with unionists. This approach, while strong on principle, failed to break a long period of stagnation and stand-off, either then or subsequently. Northern nationalists received little, if any, practical help to ameliorate their situation under continuous Unionist Party majority rule, though representations were made to Britain now and again. The activities of the IRA in England queered the pitch for any appeal to British public opinion in 1939 and subsequently.

Republicanism was formally based on a majoritarian ethos with regard to the constitutional position, while prepared to allow maximum latitude on other issues. There was a palpable sense amongst Irish nationalists as a whole of having been cheated, first by Ulster resistance to Home Rule, and then by the Boundary Commission. Neither the 1925 nor the 1938 negotiations succeeded in winning any concessions on Northern Ireland. However, when in 1940–41 there appeared to be an offer or more accurately a mirage of unity in exchange for neutrality, de Valera had grave doubts about its substance in the absence of any agreement by the Unionist government in the North (though apparently Brookeborough, not yet prime minister, was sympathetic to the idea). De Valera felt that the sacrifice of something tangible, the independence and life blood of a people, was being demanded in exchange for a probably unfulfillable promise. Like Adenauer in 1953 *vis-à-vis* a similarly elusive Soviet offer of German unity in exchange for neutrality and an abandonment of Western engagement, he refused the exchange, not least because it seriously impinged on sovereignty.[33] During the Second World War, de Valera moved resolutely against the IRA when it appeared to threaten the safety and survival of the state, albeit at the cost of deeply and permanently alienating some republicans in the process.

Towards the end of his active political career, at the Fianna Fáil *ard-fheis* of 1957, de Valera's arguments against a renewed resort to violence by the IRA were remarkably cogent, and his view on the best approach to be followed was prophetic. He said what remains true today: that there was no clear way that would inevitably end partition. He did not think force would be successful, and even if it were 'we would have left an abiding sore that would have ruined our national life for generations'. Having achieved a certain position, he continued, 'my advice to you is not to throw it all back into the melting pot'. Force had only been successful in that part of Ireland in which the IRA had had the vast majority of the people with them. Moreover, the first Dáil had been elected, not self-appointed: the IRA fought as the army of the elected government between 1919 and 1921.

On the positive side de Valera said he would welcome not

only a three-corner conference involving the two governments, but also a bilateral conference with the people of the six counties. He had come to the conclusion that the proper way to try to solve the problem of partition was to endeavour to have as close relations as possible with the people of the six counties in order to get them to combine with the people of the twenty-six counties in matters of common concern. In the case of tourism, for example, was it not obvious that the latter should combine with the people of the six counties to induce visitors to come not to the twenty-six or the six counties but to Ireland? The same applied to the marketing abroad of Irish whiskey or Irish linen. Again, was it not obvious that they should induce foreign industrialists to come to Ireland, and not to one particular part of it?[34]

The policy enunciated by Seán Lemass was a development of this position, and represented far more continuity than is generally acknowledged. Moreover his famous Oxford Union speech (in which one of the student speakers opposing him was the young Patrick Mayhew), was also prophetic of the goals that his successors up to the present would be trying to achieve. Lemass sought a statement from the British that they would like to see partition ended by agreement among the Irish, and that there was no British interest in preventing or desiring to discourage them from reaching agreement. Whilst subsequent British governments have declined to go quite that far or to act as 'persuaders for unity', they have declared their full support for agreement amongst the people of Ireland, including a willingness to legislate for unity if it has majority support, and from 1990 they disclaimed any selfish strategic or economic interest. Lemass highlighted discrimination against nationalists, but was willing to repeat the offer of devolution within a united Ireland, provided there were adequate safeguards for the ordinary rights of the nationalist minority in Northern Ireland. He stressed the value of effective economic cooperation, whether or not it led on to unity. Interestingly, behind the scenes Lord Glentoran, the Northern Ireland commerce minister, was trying without success to interest his colleagues in a free trade area, or what we would nowadays call a single market, for the island as a whole. Lemass stated his desire to see armed activities brought to an end, since they only diverted from the main issue; he observed: 'The vast majority of the Irish people support the policy of seeking the reunification of the nation along the road of cooperation leading to agreement'.[35] On the question of unionist identity and allegiance in that context, he referred favourably to Cardinal d'Alton's suggestion of an association of a united Ireland with the Commonwealth on the same basis as India, a possibility that de Valera had also sounded out with the British ambassador in Dublin in the mid-1950s.

In 1965, by meeting the prime minister of Northern Ireland Captain Terence O'Neill, Seán Lemass was at last able to put his policy into practice by seeking to advance a wide range of North–South economic cooperation. His relations were cool with the Nationalist Party, which would soon be swept aside by a younger generation for whom, in the heady days of civil rights movements and worldwide student protests, the fruits of a policy of détente and cooperation were much too slow, as well as failing to challenge head on the issue of discrimination. Perhaps, if the dialogue with O'Neill had come earlier, the effect could have allowed the charting of a different, and more peaceful, path.

The civil rights movement led to a reappraisal of republicanism all round. The peaceful revolutionary challenge to the Stormont government, anticipating by twenty years the challenges to the Communist governments of Eastern Europe in 1989, placed the Irish government in a quandary. The gradualist policy of rapprochement was superseded by events. Northern nationalists had asserted their rights without waiting any longer for leadership from Dublin. The responses to that on the part of the Irish government were of three types: to reassert the fundamental bottom line, in the hope that Irish unity might fill the vacuum created by the impending collapse of Stormont; to provide active support and assistance to a nationalist community under siege and to help them defend themselves; and to eschew any support for lethal violence, and to pursue agreement on a basis that would not only vindicate the rights of nationalists but show more understanding of unionists as they considered their long-term options.

The engagement with more militant nationalists, which might have allowed the exercise of a restraining influence, came to an abrupt end in May 1970 with the events leading to the Arms Trial; it was not resumed till 1988. The Provisional IRA, formed a few months before the trial, abandoned the heavy emphasis on socialist agitation, having seen an opening to bring down the entire edifice of partition by using traditional methods ruthlessly with modern tactics and material. A campaign conducted at first with great intensity settled into a long and brutal war of attrition. It stimulated a great deal of political activity, bringing closer together over twenty years the two governments, but not achieving the same effect on the constitutional parties. The SDLP, representing the majority of the nationalist community, is one of the few parties – along with Alliance – not to have flirted with paramilitaries at any stage; it stuck with principle to the democratic path, seeking to influence the situation and the governments as best it could, often in conditions of appalling difficulty. In the South, Fianna Fáil and other parties, whilst firmly repressing cross-border violence, pursued a peaceful political solution based on initiatives led by the two governments that would involve bringing about agreement between the constitutional parties, seeking to institute partnership or power-sharing in the North, with a strong North–South dimension. If there were differences between the parties in the South, they related mainly to questions of *de jure* acceptance of the principle of consent and of how far there should be recognition of the status quo, and of how far society in the South should be changed to meet unionist criticisms as opposed to in response to its own needs.

A strong revisionist tide in Irish historiography in relation to appalling contemporary violence went in many instances beyond critical analysis of patriotic legend to denigrate and belittle the movements, the people and the factors behind the long drive for national independence. More recently, an attempt has been made by some historians and intellectuals as well as by many political leaders to synthesise and reintegrate a proud, self-respecting and modern Irish nationalism, with new insights that are available to modernise, adapt and broaden out once more a deeply held Irish view of the world, without abandoning all fundamental values.

In the North, a political movement of growing strength developed out of and then alongside armed struggle, and has gradually established a *de facto* primacy over it. In the South, mainstream democratic or constitutional republicanism sought to establish a broad democratic and mainly nationalist consensus as an alternative to violence. It eventually succeeded, most notably in the Downing Street Declaration of 1993, in squaring the principles of self-determination and consent, taken together with the renumeration of a selfish strategic or economic interest on the part of the British government, thus providing ideological foundations for a purely political and democratic approach. Since then, the decisive factor in the shape of any new settlement is what the parties in Ireland can themselves agree. As Bertie Ahern, as the new leader of Fianna Fáil, acknowledged in 1995, 'irredentism is dead'.[36]

Recent multi-party negotiations in the North, and the balanced change on both sides of the Irish Sea to constitutional doctrines, with the ultimate choice of sovereignty to be in the future exclusively in the hands of the people of Northern Ireland, within a framework codetermined by the people of Ireland north and south, have incorporated this approach. Nationalist parties and nationalist opinion appears to endorse the approach, despite previous fundamental reservations about the principle of consent. To reach an agreement based on consent in all its aspects would help to decommission mindsets based on coercive majoritarianism requiring future political arrangements to be based in practice on at least some element of consensus between the main political traditions.

In terms of the experience of the nationalist community in the North, armed revolt against repression first by the unionists and then by the British was for many a natural reflex. But the human and political cost was huge, quite disproportionate to any progress achieved. People learned for themselves through a very costly process what Eamon de Valera could have told them in 1957 about the prospects of success. Relations between the nationalist and unionist communities, never in a good state, will be difficult and will take a long time to repair, unless there is positive and active political leadership on all sides. The disaster, which had deep roots in history, both in the twentieth century and further back, cannot just be reduced to the activities of the IRA. The responsibility must be widely spread, though without excusing the actions of any particular group.

The real question for the future is whether in the North republicanism can turn itself into a positive democratic force, capable of sustaining a purely political dynamic without further resort to the crutch of other methods that could discredit it amongst wider opinion and cripple its ability to exercise constructive political influence and engage with others. It has to take the same risk as most republicans had no choice but to take in the South in the 1920s: to forge and rely upon an effective political movement.

In the South, under the influence of booming economic conditions, a new national pride and self-confidence has burgeoned. The case against partition is no longer so much that a vital arm has been cut off. It is now more a matter of the power of mutual economic attraction and the operation of market forces in a wider European and global context. Further progress is required before fully favourable economic conditions for Irish unity will exist, but there is every merit in mutually beneficial North–South cooperation and integration, and without prejudice to other economic benefits for the time being of the British connection. The social, cultural and sectarian obstacles to understanding can no longer be asserted with much plausibility to originate or exist mainly in the South. The political differences are now pretty much down to the core element of contesting senses of identity, Irish and British, and to also the natural fears of a minority community on the island of Ireland.

Historically, the Protestant/unionist community in Ireland had, at different times, three options. The first and most favoured option was to establish and defend an ascendancy. The second option, when that was no longer possible, was to retreat without positive engagement and to remain apart. The third option was to work with those of the nationalist tradition to forge an Ireland that would reflect the best in all traditions, in an enlightened and democratic spirit and out of a deep attachment to a shared country. Modern Ireland owes a huge debt to the vision of individuals from all backgrounds and traditions, but there is no doubt that people like Swift, Grattan, Tone, Emmet, Davis, Mitchel, Parnell and Yeats and many others played a formative role with their contemporaries in paving the way for or forging a modern Irish nation-state, with the intention that it would be open to all traditions on the island on a non-majoritarian basis. The reality perhaps fell well short of that in the early difficult stages of the new state, but there has been a gradual return to a broader vision.

Today, it is an open question, as well as a challenge, learning from both the inspiration and the mistakes of the past, as to whether the nationalist and unionist traditions can overcome the deep distrust of the past and build a future on this island together rather than separately, back to back. The task may seem difficult or even impossible. But is there any real alternative, and will we not have to keep returning to it, until a basis for living in harmony can be achieved? We need a settled conviction that the only way in which the true republican ideal in Ireland can be achieved is by vindicating and adhering to democracy in the fullest sense and through sensible and pragmatic compromise that allows ample space for others. Democracy provides guarantees to no one, but opportunities for everyone through the power of persuasion. There are no historical inevitabilities that relieve any of us of our responsibility.

## NOTES

1 P.H. Pearse, 'The Separatist Idea', in his *The Murder Machine and other essays* (Cork, 1976), pp. 45–61.
2 P.H. Pearse, *Plays, Stories, Poems* (Dublin, 1980), p. 336.
3 *The Memoirs of Desmond FitzGerald* (London, 1968), pp. 140–1, 143. FitzGerald also records how he was angered and depressed by notes dated the 1st (or 2nd etcetera) day of the republic, not least 'because that method of dating seemed to associate the rising with the French Revolution, an association that was utterly repugnant to me'.
4 Nicholas Mansergh, *The Irish Question 1840-1921* (London, 1975), p. 28.
5 P.H. Pearse, 'The Spiritual Nation', in his *The Murder Machine and other essays* (Cork, 1976), p. 76.
6 Seán Lemass, speech of April 1965, cited in John Horgan, *Seán Lemass: The Enigmatic Patriot* (Dublin, 1997), p. 208.
7 'Easter 1916', *The Collected Poems of W.B. Yeats* (London, 1963), p. 205.
8 Cope's telegram to T.J., 3 September 1921, in Thomas Jones, *Whitehall Diary Volume III Ireland 1918–1925* edited by Keith Middlemas (London, 1971), p. 105.
9 Florence O'Donoghue, *No Other Law* (Dublin, 1954), p. 181.
10 *Iris Dháil Eireann. Official Report, Debate on the Treaty between Great Britain and Ireland signed in London on the 6th December 1921*, cols. 113, 118.
11 Cited in Michael O'Sullivan, *Seán Lemass: A Biography* (Tallaght, 1994), p. 38.
12 Brian P. Murphy, *Patrick Pearse and the Lost Republican Ideal* (Dublin, 1991), p. 182.
13 Plato, *The Republic*, translated by A.D. Lindsay (London and New York, 1964), p. 24.
14 Thomas N. Mitchell, *Cicero the Senior Statesman* (New Haven and London, 1991), p. 63.
15 *Thomas Paine's Common Sense: The Call to Independence* edited by Thomas Wendel (New York, 1975), pp. 61–6.
16 W.A. Maguire (ed.), *Kings in Conflict: The Revolutionary War in Ireland and Its Aftermath 1689–1750* (Belfast, 1990), p. 56.
17 *Iris Dháil Eireann. Official Report, Debate on the Treaty . . .*, col. 178.
18 Theobald Wolfe Tone, *An Argument on behalf of the Catholics of Ireland* (reprinted Belfast, 1973), p. 30.
19 C.V. Wedgwood, *William the Silent* (London, 1955).
20 John Locke, *Two Treatises of Government*, edited by Peter Laslett (New York and London, 1960).
21 Montesquieu, *De l'esprit des lois*, edited by Gonzague Truc (Paris, 1961).

22 Jean-Jacques Rousseau, *Du contrat social*, edited by Pierre Burgelin (Paris, 1966), pp. 1, 108, 112.
23 Anthony Carty, *Was Ireland Conquered? International Law and the Irish Question* (Laden, 1996), pp. 109–12.
24 Jacques Godechot (ed.), *Les Constitutions de la France depuis 1789* (Paris, 1970), pp. 33–5.
25 *Memoirs of Theobald Wolfe Tone*, edited by W.T.W. Tone (London, 1827), vol ii, pp. 35–6.
26 Cited and translated from Bernard Bergerot, *Lazare Hoche* (Paris, 1988).
27 Jefferson to Governor John Langdon, 5 March 1810, in Adrienne Koche and William Peden (eds.) *The Life and Selected Writings of Thomas Jefferson* (New York, 1972), pp. 603–4.
28 Brigitte Harmann, *Elisabeth: Kaiserin wider Willen* (Munich, 1993), pp. 11–12, 63.
29 Edmund Burke, *Reflections on the Revolution in France*, edited by Conor Cruise O'Brien (Harmondsworth, 1968), pp. 169–70.
30 Immanuel Kant, 'Zum ewigen Frieden–Ein philosophischer Entwurf' in *Kants sämmtliche Werke*, vol. 6, edited by G. Hartenstein (Leipzig, 1868), pp. 406–36.
31 Hubert Henry, *A History of Latin America from the Beginnings to the Present* (London, 1984), pp. 554–5.
32 Cited in Horgan, *Seán Lemass*, p. 295.
33 Paul Canning, *British Policy towards Ireland 1921–1941* (Oxford, 1985), pp. 262–317.
34 De Valera, speech to the Fianna Fáil *ard-fheis*, 19 November 1957, in *Speeches and Statements by Eamon de Valera 1917–1973*, edited by Maurice Moynihan (Dublin and New York, 1980), pp. 580–6.
35 Seán Lemass, 'One Nation', speech to the Oxford Union Society, 15 October 1959, cited from *The Story of Fianna Fáil: First Phase* (Dublin, 1960), pp. 108–16.
36 Bertie Ahern, speech to the Irish Association, 2 February 1995.

# 3

# The Irish Republican Ideal

### MITCHEL McLAUGHLIN

Human progress has come about because men and women dared to dream of ways to make a better world. The same can be said for political progress: that it was the men and women who dared to dream of change who influenced the development of political thought. Where they saw tyranny they sought its overthrow, where they saw injustice they sought justice, where they saw conflict they sought peace, and where they saw inequality and division they sought equality and unity. At different times, for different generations, the issues to be faced and the problems to be overcome varied enormously, yet the unwavering impulse to achieve change for the better has been the essence of positive political activity.

Throughout the history of humankind, people have ordered their affairs, or had their affairs ordered for them, in a variety of ways. There have been tribal societies, monarchies, systems based upon slavery, upon feudalism or upon tyranny. Chieftains, kings and queens or aristocratic, political or military elites have governed nations. Much of the world's history until relatively recently has been of the few ruling the many. The story of most countries today is of the struggle by the many to obtain their freedom. In many regions across the world, considerable progress has yet to be made before it can truthfully be said that liberty, the birthright of every person, has replaced political oppression. It is clear that the impulse to achieve change for the better is as relevant today as it ever was.

Definitions of democracy have varied from age to age. Precisely who should be entitled to political power and who should be excluded from it are questions that have dominated political affairs the world over. The modern concept of democracy, with universal suffrage and an electorate that chooses its political representatives in regular plebiscites, is only a very recent phenomenon in historical terms. What we take for granted today was achieved by men and women who refused to believe that the world had to stay as it was. Rather than live within the limits of social, political and economic structures designed for the benefit of a minority, they fought for structures that would be of benefit to all. They did this in the face of determined and frequently brutal opposition from their rulers and from those interest groups that benefited from the maintenance of the status quo.

In Ireland the conviction that it should be the people of Ireland alone who manage their own affairs has a long and honourable pedigree. Even though the Gaelic Irish were accustomed to thinking in terms governed by the concepts of aristocratic rule and kingship, they were equally aware that English interference in Irish affairs would ultimately lead to the destruction of the Irish people and their culture. As far back as 1599, Hugh O'Neill was demanding that Ireland be granted the status of an independent country, nominally under the English crown but effectively governed by the Irish alone. He actually used the word 'republic' to describe his vision of an independent Ireland, although at that time the word was generally understood to mean 'state' and had none of the connotations of modern republicanism.

The political debates that had been triggered in Ireland as a consequence of the American Revolution became even more animated following the French Revolution of 1789. Most Irish Presbyterians were in sympathy with the American revolutionaries, whose ranks contained many Presbyterians who had fled from Ireland seeking freedom of conscience. The issues over which the American Revolution was fought also struck a chord in Ireland: the control exercised by Westminster over its colonies was increasingly viewed as despotic. The British defeat in America and the overthrow of the French *ancien régime* were proof not only that ordinary people could organise their own system of government but also that political systems could be changed by popular revolt. People became aware that the way things were could be challenged and changed. Freedom from control by the few was possible, and the message of '*liberté, égalité, fraternité*' presented major challenges to those seeking reform.

Ireland's radicals, in common with radical thinkers throughout most of Europe, believed that a new era was dawning that would see people regulate their affairs upon principles of liberty and equality. They sought the abolition of privileges and corruption and the reshaping of institutions of state in accordance with the rights and wishes of 'the people'. Following the loss of the American colonies, the idea of an Ireland completely separated from Westminster control was no longer unthinkable. At the end of the eighteenth century, Ireland's population was almost 5 million, America's was roughly 2 million, while the population of Britain was around 9 million. The economic potential of an independent Ireland enjoying friendly relations with both America and Europe was not inconsiderable, and whilst those seeking reforms were not initially motivated by separatist ideas, the issue of separatism came to feature more prominently in political debate as the century drew to a close.

In part this was a result of the response from Westminster to calls for reform in Ireland. Fear of separation had led, in the

1780s, to the emergence of an Irish unionist coterie that sought union with the Westminster parliament. Certain elements of the ruling elite in Ireland feared that their power and privilege would be swept away if the reforms being called for were implemented. Among moderates the objective was partial, not full, freedom for the Irish people. Nor were certain of Ireland's interest groups alone in their fears about progressive change, as is shown by this extract from a letter written in 1791 by the Irish chief secretary, Hobart, to the British home secretary:

> The connection between England and Ireland rests absolutely upon the Protestant ascendancy: abolish distinctions, and you create a Catholic superiority. If you are to maintain a Protestant ascendancy, it must be by substituting influence for numbers. Whilst you maintain the Protestant ascendancy, the ruling powers in Ireland look to England as the foundation of their authority and influence. The Executive Government of both countries must ever (as it has always been) be under the same control.

Certain English statesmen were less concerned with a union of the Irish and Westminster parliaments than they were with another kind of union: that between the people of Ireland. In 1791 also, the foreign minister, Lord Grenville, wrote to Lord Westmoreland, the lord lieutenant of Ireland:

> I cannot help feeling a very great anxiety that such measures may be taken as may effectually counteract the union between the Catholics and Dissenters, at which the latter are evidently aiming. I may be a false prophet, but there is no evil that I would not prophesy if that union takes place at the present moment.

The idea of Presbyterians and Catholics joining together to oppose the establishment likewise appalled Hugh Boulter, the Church of Ireland archbishop of Armagh, who wrote: 'The worst of this is that it stands to unite Protestant and Papist, and whenever that happens, goodbye to the English interest in Ireland forever.' The reason for such fears was the emergence in

Ireland of a new brand of political thought: Irish republicanism. It was a political philosophy based upon the belief that the people of Ireland should set aside their religious differences and act together for the common good. It envisaged the people of Ireland alone making decisions about their destiny.

The background to the alarm of the Ascendancy elite and of British politicians lay specifically in the establishment of a new political club in Belfast in 1791. Its founding members were a small secret committee of eleven Presbyterian businessmen. The publication, in September 1791, of a pamphlet entitled *An Argument on Behalf of the Catholics of Ireland* drew their attention to its author, Theobald Wolfe Tone. Tone was a close friend of Thomas Russell, who had been associated with those who were to form the club when he was an officer of the British army stationed in Belfast the year before. Both Tone and Russell were invited to Belfast by the Presbyterian group, and the meeting led within days to the foundation of a new society, on 14 October 1791, which they called the Society of United Irishmen. It was an entirely constitutional and legal organisation, formed, as stated in the first sentence of its constitution, 'for the purpose of forwarding a brotherhood of affection, a communion of rights, and a union of power among Irishmen of every religious persuasion, and thereby to obtain a complete reform in the legislature founded on the principles of civil, political, and religious liberty'. Three weeks later the society's Dublin branch was founded. The minutes of the Dublin meeting included the following:

> ... we have agreed to form a society called The Society of United Irishmen, and we do pledge ourselves to our country, and mutually to each other, that we will steadily support, and endeavour by all due means to carry into effect the following resolutions;
>
> Resolved that the weight of English influence in the government of this country is so great as to require a cordial union among all the people of Ireland, to maintain that balance which is essential to the preservation of our liberties and the extension of our commerce.

That the sole constitutional mode by which this influence can be opposed is by a complete and radical reform of the representation of the people in Parliament.

That no reform is practicable, efficacious, or just which shall not include Irishmen of every religious persuasion.

We have gone to what we perceive to be the root of the evil. We have stated what we conceive to be the remedy. With a Parliament thus reformed, everything is easy, without it nothing can be done. And we do call on, and most earnestly exhort our fellow countrymen in general to follow our example and form similar societies in every quarter of the kingdom for the promotion of constitutional knowledge, the abolition of bigotry in religion and politics, and the equal distribution of the rights of man throughout all sects and denominations of Irishmen.

The United Irishmen, with their egalitarian ideals and goals, remain the most progressive political force ever to have emerged in Ireland. Their constitution and discussions incited no violence or revolution; rather, they called for reform, the abolition of bigotry and religion in politics, and the equal distribution of voting and other rights throughout all sects and denominations of Irishmen. From the vantage point of today (and making due allowance for the sexist bias of the times), the brilliance of what the United Irishmen sought and how they set about trying to obtain it still shine out like a beacon from the past, their message still having the power to illuminate the present and guide our way forward into the future.

However, the British government of the day had neither time nor use for non-sectarian politics in Ireland. The interests of the Ascendancy clique through whom England's political will was imposed upon Ireland were deemed to be of paramount importance. Having deemed the United Irishmen to be potential traitors, the British government set about ensuring both that the organisation would have no place in political life and that its spokesmen would be denied the freedom to peaceably advance their political beliefs. In Ireland a vicious circle was initiated in which the government attempted to repress any manifestation of popular opinion by either Catholics or Dissenters. As coercion followed attempted conciliation, there was inevitably a hardening of resistance by the United Irishmen, who in most cases had begun as constitutional reformers but were now driven by events to become underground physical-force revolutionaries.

General Knox, commander of the British army in Dungannon, made his intentions plain in a letter to General Lake, the army commander in Ulster:

> I have arranged a plan to scour a district full of unregistered arms, or said to be so and this I do, not so much with a hope to succeed to any extent, as to increase the animosity between the Orangemen and the United Irishmen. Upon that animosity depends the safety of the centre counties of the North.

A reign of terror began, with raids, show trials and executions. Soldiers stationed in Belfast 'were encouraged by their officers and magistrates to take the law into their own hands and attack anyone they suspected of democratic or republican sympathies'. The United Irishmen, who it must be remembered had started out with no aim other than to bring about a decent and just society in Ireland, were hunted and terrorised until eventually they were left with no option but to fight back.

French help, when it arrived, was too little, too late, and the United Irishmen, poorly armed, poorly trained and poorly organised, were eventually no match for trained troops with cavalry and artillery. Over 30,000 people died during the various bouts of fighting that took place in Ireland in 1798, in part because the British government of the day put its own military analysis above the right of all of the people of Ireland to govern their own affairs. The United Irish dead included Catholics, Protestants and Dissenters, killed fighting for their lives and their republic. Shortly afterwards, members of the Irish parliament were bribed into doing away with their own legislature, and the Act of Union was passed in 1800.

Clearly the Union was not a suitable political structure for dealing with Ireland's problems or for advancing the aspirations of the Irish people. The futility of engaging in constitutional political activity was exposed time and time again. The Young Ireland movement of the 1840s marked a re-emergence of the republican tradition. As with the United Irishmen of the 1790s, many of the movement's leaders were Protestants, their message of equality and independence as valid as it ever was. Keeping faith with the United Irish ideal of eliminating bigotry, the Young Irelanders called for integrated education, a concept that has become increasingly popular in recent times. The British response to demands for an end to sectarianism, for equality and for self-government was the familiar one of harassment, arrests and transportations.

The Fenian movement of the late 1850s was another republican attempt to secure independence, this time, in view of the absence of effective politics, one based purely on military lines. Despite failing in their armed endeavours, the Fenians successfully established a revolutionary political movement and a militant socio-cultural pressure group, involved in land agitation, sport and Irish language revival. They furthermore formed an influential interest lobby in US affairs.

Asquith's refusal to impose Home Rule on Ulster, together with Lloyd George's promise to Carson in 1916 that parts of Ulster would be excluded from any Home Rule act, demonstrated clearly that the British government had no intention of satisfying the democratically expressed will of the people of Ireland. In the nineteenth and early part of the twentieth centuries the majority of the people of Ireland had peacefully used the democratic process to advance their case for reform. But the British government bowed to the threat of violence made by a minority; as was noted in the report of the New Ireland Forum (1984): 'The message – which was not lost on unionists – was that a threat to use violence would succeed. To the nationalists, the conclusion was that the democratic constitutional process was not to be allowed to be effective.'

The democratic will of the Irish people having been ignored, and in the absence of any understanding by the British that prostituting political principles was a recipe for violent conflict, republican forces rose in rebellion. Even after the Easter Rising was suppressed and opinion in nationalist Ireland hardened, British statesmen continued to urge that partition be accepted and were not averse to coercing the majority of Ireland's people to achieve that end. The 1918 general election, the last all-Ireland plebiscite, saw Sinn Féin win 73 of the 105 Irish seats, yet still the will of the majority was ignored. Further conflict and loss of life ensued between 1919 and 1921, when eventually the majority were coerced into accepting the partition of their country under the threat of 'immediate and terrible war'. While British politicians said that unionists would not be coerced into a united Ireland, they had no compunction about coercing nationalists into the new six-county statelet, which was a geographical entity carved out solely to ensure unionist domination. Carson himself explained to the British House of Commons on 18 March 1920, the reason why unionists only demanded six counties of Ulster:

> The truth is that we came to the conclusion after many anxious hours and anxious days of going into the whole matter almost parish by parish and townland by townland that you would have no chance of successfully starting a parliament in Belfast which was to be responsible for the government of Donegal, Cavan and Monaghan. We should like to have the very largest area possible, naturally. The figures will at once show where the difficulties come in. We have to refer in these matters to Protestant and Catholic because these are really the burning questions over there: while you would leave out seventy thousand [Protestants] who are in these three counties, you would bring from these three counties into the Northern province an additional two hundred and sixty thousand Roman Catholics.

The result of the British-imposed partition was civil war in the South and pogroms and sectarian hatred in the North. The suppression of the republican ideal resulted in Britain maintaining a strategic presence in Ireland, and the retarding of natural economic, political, social and cultural development on both sides of the border. The sectarian nature of the northern statelet is well documented.

As we have seen, over the centuries political development in Ireland was traditionally dictated by Crown considerations, and the garrison elite there controlled the country in Britain's interests. As a consequence, religious and cultural differences were used to create a form of social and political apartheid. The consequent social and economic problems and related conflict were a direct result of this inequality. British interference meant that a healthy democracy failed to develop and religious differences were exploited as a means of maintaining control. Self-determination was denied, sectional interests were pandered to, British military and economic interests were deemed paramount, and the constant failure of constitutional politics to redress very real grievances left the resort to arms as the only viable option for a people trying to gain control over their own destinies.

The only occasion when the British state failed to crush ruthlessly armed resistance in Ireland came in 1914, when Ulster unionists were permitted to impede the democratic process by force of arms. As a consequence of the denial of progressive political development, the potential for violent political conflict in Ireland has been ever-present since partition. It is clear, employing the political standards of today, that British rule in Ireland was unjust and that it served to perpetuate an abnormal society. The continued existence of a British-controlled part of Ireland founded on sectarian considerations and governed in an unjust and coercive manner is a political anachronism today. Republicans have been to the forefront in challenging the injustices that are a feature of life in the six counties, and we believe that it is a republican solution that will yet provide the answers to those problems.

During more than fifty years of one-party rule at Stormont, it was very obvious that neither constitutional Irish nationalism nor the various Irish governments throughout that period had effectively countered the discrimination and repression experienced by the northern nationalist community. The North functioned throughout that period as a unionist state for a unionist population. Many people who knew the truth about the excesses of one-party unionist rule chose to close their eyes and say nothing. The indifference of the majority of Westminster and Leinster House politicians demonstrated the failure of the political process and led many in our society to resort once again to armed struggle to oppose state violence.

Moreover, the second-class citizenship of the nationalist community was never seriously examined or effectively challenged by 'constitutional nationalism' subsequently, throughout the twenty-five years of direct rule. Yet it is arguable that their conditions actually worsened from 1969. The attempt by the Stormont administration to crush by force the popular uprising by nationalists across the six counties, the occupation of nationalist areas by the British army, and the resistance to this by nationalists and republicans set the scene for a bloody conflict during which more than three thousand people lost their lives, thousands more were imprisoned, and society became militarised.

For thirty years, as each year gave way to another, the conflict deepened. As the loss of life continued and as human tragedy piled on top of tragedy, a deep sense of despair gripped people and politicians alike. By the late eighties it was clear that there was a political and military stalemate. British generals who had been fighting the IRA since 1970 publicly accepted what everyone else knew: they could not defeat the IRA. Sinn Féin president Gerry Adams accepted this also and argued for those who were calling on the IRA to end their military campaign to provide an alternative route for republicans to achieve their objectives. Also in the late eighties, dialogue between the SDLP and Sinn Féin explored such an alternative through several meetings between both parties. Although these meetings did not produce the alternative, they laid the foundation for fresh thinking among republicans and nationalists. A number of years and many hundreds more people's deaths were to pass before another, more sustained effort was made to put together an alternative, based this time on a tripartite nationalist consensus: Hume–Adams–Reynolds.

The search for a nationalist consensus was influenced not just by events in Ireland but also by developments abroad. Outside Ireland the winds of change were blowing in other seemingly insoluble conflicts. Events in South Africa and the Middle East cast their long shadow over Irish affairs. As change unfolded there the unthinkable began to be thought about by republicans and nationalists. Hence by mid-1993 Hume and Adams had reached agreement on a process that both believed could lead to lasting peace in Ireland. A nationalist consensus was beginning to take shape which would break the mould of the Irish/British conflict.

The Hume–Adams agreement began a process which was strengthened when the Irish government led by Albert Reynolds came on board. In turn important players in Irish-American society also became a part of that consensus. The peace process was built on the following agreed positions:

(1) that the people of Ireland have the right to exercise national self-determination.
(2) that the people of Ireland are divided at present on how that right is to be exercised.
(3) that Stormont rule was undemocratic, exclusionist and discriminatory.
(4) that no solution is possible within the six counties.
(5) that the status quo of direct rule is not an option for a democratic future.
(6) that we all subscribed, with different emphasis of course, to the political option of a united Ireland.
(7) that we all recognised the changes that are already under way in our society and that such change should be managed in the interests of all the people of Ireland. Whilst it is obvious that these understandings have had a radical effect on nationalist parties, differences remain on the origins of social and economic problems and on how to resolve them. However, the despair of the years before the first IRA cessation of August 1994 have been replaced with hope and expectation. The public unity between

Gerry Adams, John Hume and the various *taoisigh*, especially Reynolds and Ahern, have generated a strong, confident and assertive nationalist people, particularly in the six counties.

The Irish peace process emerged because of the nationalist consensus. If the peace process is to succeed the nationalist consensus will have to move to defend it from those who would separate or divide us. We must defend it and ensure that eventually the full potential of a lasting, durable and democratic settlement is found within the negotiations.

Partition has failed – this is a common position within the nationalist consensus. Its failure is demonstrated by the history of conflict and division that has riven Irish society. Tinkering with the status quo will not resolve the violence and instability that are inherent in the six-county statelet. A combined focus will ensure consistent progress and will be vital to the continued development of the peace process. Peace in Ireland will be achieved when the political parties can agree and form a government of national consensus. Sinn Féin's mission is to point the way.

Good will and political commitment will be essential elements in the search for an agreed and inclusive settlement in Ireland. Lateral thinking and common sense must also prevail. All the political parties must be prepared to consider, in a flexible and creative manner, the ideas of others. Sinn Féin has always argued for a united Ireland and that partition, by any democratic standards, has been inimical to the best interests of the people of Ireland. The Sinn Féin analysis has rested primarily on the democratic principle of national self-determination in Ireland, on the denial of that right by successive British governments, and on the tragic record of discrimination, division, conflict and death that has resulted.

STRATEGIC INTERESTS

Britain's role as a world power has diminished to a remarkable degree since the 1920s and this, allied to the ending of the Cold

War, has affected those historical strategic imperatives that hitherto have dictated the relationship between Britain and Ireland. In recent years it has become possible for British cabinet ministers to disclaim any selfish strategic or economic interest in Ireland. This is a most welcome statement, particularly if the present process of dialogue can be developed to the point where the British government also ends its political interest.

In Ireland, the policies of the European Union are increasingly impacting in an all-island context. Social and economic harmonisation has to a considerable degree already removed any rational justification for two systems of government on such a small island. Two economic systems, two transportation systems, two health systems: we have two of everything, including two of the highest rates of unemployment and social deprivation in the EU. Yet an apparently impervious mindset acts to deflect the intrinsic dynamic for change in all of this.

The twin disciplines of competition with other economies and of the overwhelming desire to face into a stable and democratic future must eventually compel the political parties in Ireland to address the inherent instability and the inefficiency of the present constitutional arrangements. Other factors are also commanding attention as we approach the end of this most turbulent century.

DEMOGRAPHICS

The demographic trends as reflected in the 1991 census figures clearly point to an ever-increasing nationalist population and a decreasing unionist population. This has led to increasing tension and instability as the unionist community contemplates losing ever more political control and power in the six counties.

The next census, in 2001, will undoubtedly confirm this demographic trend. These developments are effectively eroding the ability of unionists to exercise their veto over political change in numerous areas of political life. Already four of the six counties, Fermanagh, Tyrone, Derry and latterly Armagh have actual and increasing nationalist majorities. Unionists have lost political control of Belfast, hitherto the capital of unionism, as well as of Derry and numerous towns. This reality should encourage new thinking on all sides.

THE COMMON GROUND

Despite their many differences, common ground between nationalists and unionists does exist. For example, which government, political party or leader would any longer deny that the former Stormont regime was undemocratic in its conception and in its practices? Few, if any. The question of consent was neither an issue nor a principle in those days. And which government, political party or leader would defend the current status quo as the democratic model for our future? Not even Ian Paisley or Robert McCartney. Does this not indicate that there exists a potentially significant consensus across the full spectrum of political opinion in Ireland: on the political failures of the past, on current political realities, and on the consequent need for change? Political leaders and the political process must demonstrate that there is an effective alternative to conflict. They must devise a constitutional and political framework through a democratic process of negotiation that will accommodate and manage change.

A crucially important question must be addressed in the course of political negotiations. The question could be framed in the following manner: will there be a united Ireland? All parties, whether nationalist/republican or unionist, and both governments must contribute to resolving this question.

Of course there are very many people, and not all of them from within the unionist community, who will argue that a united Ireland will never happen and that the only viable solution is a modern variation of partition with in-built and democratic safeguards within the existing constitutional arrangements. We will listen to these points of view.

However, ask this question of any nationalist in any part of Ireland and the diaspora, and they will answer, 'Yes, I strongly believe that there will be a united Ireland.' Obviously within the unionist community there are those who also believe this and thus, however reluctantly, share the view of an overwhelming majority of opinion on this island. The debate on whether a united Ireland is currently on the political horizon is often characterised by disagreement about when and how unification is likely to develop, not if it is going to happen.

The fear of change is a well-known and understandable reaction. It is especially so when cultural, national and religious identity is perceived to be at risk. But the central question of whether a united Ireland is going to emerge must be comprehensively answered. Only when that happens will it be possible to avoid the zero-sum conundrum. An open discussion in Britain as well as Ireland on the question, will there be a united Ireland? is an indispensable requirement for a settlement. For the purposes of that debate, the issue of when and how a united Ireland might emerge should be addressed separately and subsequently.

This approach to the core political issue would create a non-threatening opportunity for all sections of society to participate in a democratic consideration of this crucial matter. It would thus be possible for all those who have an interest or opinion about this matter to assemble their definitive arguments, and thus identify and explore all the democratic possibilities.

Democratic opinion must seek to change British government policy from one of upholding the union to one of ending the union. Nationalists and republicans must seek to convince unionists that a united Ireland is the desirable and inevitable outcome of global, European and national developments.

It is sometimes contended that the continuation of the Union does not and will not prejudice the right of nationalists in the North of Ireland to regard themselves as being Irish or as being part of the Irish nation. Indeed, the very fact that there is a vibrant nationalist community in the North of Ireland seventy-five years after partition clearly demonstrates that the mere fact of the Union did not deprive nationalists of their sense of Irish identity. Irish identity exists even though there is no political union with the rest of the island. It is a paradox of the northern situation that the sense of Irish identity held by the nationalist community in the North has thrived. The growth in the use of the Irish language, the growth and strength of the GAA, the support for the Republic of Ireland soccer team by nationalist youth, and the pervasive display of nationalist regalia in nationalist areas are clear testimony to the vibrancy of the sense of Irish identity. A burgeoning and confident Catholic middle class has maintained its sense of Irishness notwithstanding improved economic circumstances. The fact that 40 per cent of the electorate vote for nationalist and/or republican parties in the North of Ireland – and that this number of voters is on an upward trend – speaks for itself.

For its part, the unionist community clings with great intensity to its sense of British identity and it does so in circumstances where it perceives the political union with Britain as a *sine qua non* of its viability as a separate community on this island. Yet the role of the Union as the defining element of an identity is in marked contrast to the role of the Irish nation. Unionists seem to convey an impression of being confused about their sense of national identity and exude a feeling of being threatened by political developments beyond their exclusive control. This apprehension on their part occurs as a phenomenon notwithstanding the fact of the union with Britain. One must pose a number of questions. Why is it that nationalism in the North thrives without a constitutional link with the South, yet unionists perceive a constitutional link as the bottom line of their survival? Why is the fact of a political union indispensable to the unionist sense of British identity but unnecessary for the sense of an Irish identity?

The unionist sense of identity is primarily one-dimensional. Without the Union the unionists, as a separate community, believe they will cease to exist. This belief in itself could contain the seed of their destruction in the event that the union ends or is radically transformed. To ensure the survival of the unionists' sense of identity in a post-Union society, unionism should seek to broaden its view of the elements that constitute its sense of a separate identity. That British identity is a matrix of connecting factors that tie the unionists into the broader British family. Among these connecting factors are the strong historical and family ties among the Ascendancy, shared religious beliefs, shared military experience in two world wars and many imperial wars, a common language, and a broadly similar set of moral values (shared particularly with Tory England). All these connecting factors contribute to the British identity that is cherished by unionists. Equally, the northern nationalist community possesses connecting factors with the rest of Ireland that contribute to the nationalists' sense of identity; it is the fact of the existence of these connecting factors that principally constitutes their identity.

Simply to look at a given constitutional arrangement and to see that as the only or primary basis of a communal identity is a fatal mistake for unionism. The error of unionist politics has been to equate their identity with a continuing political union and to use the fact of this union as a litmus test of that identity's survival. Thus, should a very slim majority of inhabitants in the North of Ireland opt for a unitary state then a significant unionist minority would forfeit everything. Change would become a zero-sum game with one set of winners and one set of losers. If unionists were to find that they could become a minority within the North of Ireland it is difficult to believe that they would not resist such change violently. Indeed such an epochal event would, in all probability, be preceded by massive sectarian strife initiated by loyalist paramilitaries engaged in a heroic last stand for the Union and unionism. The one-dimensional approach by the unionist community to its sense of identity is inimical to efforts to create an agreed Ireland. The principle of consent based on a majoritarian approach simply helps to underscore this one-dimensional approach to the unionists' British identity. To build or sustain a political identity on a fossilised sense of the union with Britain is political short-sightedness in more than one respect. The Britain of 1800 or 1920 is not the Britain that exists at the end of this millennium. Rather, Britain is a multiracial society with a weakening attachment to church and crown. The Westminster parliament is itself no longer all-powerful or the sole repository of sovereignty in respect of Britain and the North of Ireland. To maintain such a limited identity is to preclude an agreement with nationalist Ireland. Any agreement on the future of the six counties must be preceded by the absence of absolute positions. It is only a refocused sense of unionist identity that can move away from an absolutist requirement for the Union in its present form.

THE INTERPLAY OF SEVERAL UNIONS

There already exists another political union affecting the North of Ireland that cannot be ignored. The European Union (EU), through its commission, parliament, and its court, day in and day out exercises legislative, executive and judicial powers that apply to the North of Ireland. Any view of the Union that ignores this reality is a dangerous anachronism. Indeed through the European Union, Irish citizens have input into the affairs of the North of Ireland in a number of ways. It was particularly instructive recently to be listening to a European Commission official expounding the policy of the EU in relation to the BSE crisis in the UK. Irish citizens hold and have held office as commissioners of the European Union and indeed as judges of the European Court, and their decisions, individually and collectively, have directly affected the interests of the North of Ireland and its citizens. At present the entire island of Ireland elects representatives to the European Parliament who, specifically in areas of agriculture, liaise with one another.

Moreover, there is not simply another political union with Europe: there is also a geographical/physical union with the rest of Ireland. This physical union with the rest of Ireland is becoming closer day in and day out with the development of a single island economy and an infrastructure to facilitate that development.

Life in the North of Ireland involves the daily interactive play of three separate unions, namely the political union with Britain, the political union with the European Union, and the geographical and physical union with the rest of Ireland. To focus on only one of these unions and isolate that as the sole determinant of the North of Ireland's future and to so determine relations within these islands is a narrow and bankrupt approach to the peaceful coexistence of nationalists and unionists on the island of Ireland.

By definition a one-dimensional approach to a British identity dictates that unionism determines its relationship with the rest of the people of Ireland in terms of the continued existence of the union with Britain. In doing so, unionism is putting itself at the mercy of a British government and a changing British people. Indeed, the Union so cherished by unionism is itself no more than a voluntary association of England, Wales, Scotland and the North of Ireland. Changes in devolution in Scotland may lead to Scottish independence and in turn a sundering of the Union. In Wales it is less clear where devolution is going. Voluntary detachment by the North of Ireland's other partners in the Union cannot be prevented by unionism – the Union could be ended without unionism being able to stop this. Its cherished Union is only as strong as the desire of England, Scotland and Wales to remain in a political union with the North of Ireland. A guarantee given by the Westminster parliament can be revoked by any other Westminster parliament. If unionists want security – and thus not to be exposed to the vicissitudes of British interests in Ireland – a historic compromise with Irish nationalism is required. That can only be achieved by negotiations that examine and provide for all the elements of a community's identity. The assertion of an absolute and unconditional right to a political union will not produce an agreed Ireland. It is only by focusing on all the unions and on the multiplicity of connecting factors that a compromise can be achieved between nationalists and unionists that will stand the test of time.

As we approach the bicentenary of the United Irishmen's gallant attempt to create a true democracy in Ireland we would do well to remember their guiding principles. The Society of United Irishmen was founded 'for the purpose of forwarding a brotherhood of affection, a communion of rights, and a union of power among Irishmen of every religious persuasion, and thereby to obtain a complete reform in the legislature founded on the principles of civil, political, and religious liberty'. The objection to the 'weight of English influence in the government of this country', the belief that 'the sole constitutional mode by which this influence can be opposed is by a complete and radical reform of the representation of the people in Parliament', and the acknowledgement that 'no reform is practicable, efficacious, or just which shall not include Irishmen of every religious persuasion' are sentiments that are as relevant to our situation today as they ever were. And who can object to the aspiration to work for 'the abolition of bigotry in religion and politics, and the equal distribution of the rights of man throughout all sects and denominations of Irishmen'? Power vested in sectional interests is no solution, power dependent upon coercion is no solution, discrimination and oppression and intolerance and prejudice are not the hallmarks of a healthy progressive society. Equality, which is both the principle underlying republican beliefs and the republican solution, is the key to overcoming all those ills.

What sort of society do republicans want? One where no grouping dominates others by virtue of holding particular religious or cultural affiliations. One where economic opportunities are available to all, irrespective of creed or political loyalties. The right to live one's life according to one's own particular culture should be guaranteed to all. With rights come responsibilities however, and the freedom to celebrate one's culture should not be abused by intolerance of the rights of others. The institutions governing society must be open to all, and representative of all. The law must not be used as an instrument to coerce and dominate any section of society, and those charged with upholding and maintaining the law must be drawn from all sections of society. The needs and aspirations of the people of Ireland should be subservient to no other interests.

A number of prominent British politicians have stated that Britain no longer has any selfish or strategic interests in Ireland.

Republicans want to see the social, economic and cultural damage that partition has wreaked upon this island repaired. Our links across the border – often with our own kith and kin – give us an obvious interest in all-Ireland structures that can enable us to develop solutions to problems old and new. Economic necessity requires that we coordinate activities around areas such as agriculture, fisheries, transport, tourism, communications systems, energy, research and development, and job creation. Our shared heritage means that environmental issues are of common concern. Aspects of shared culture are also of common concern. Issues that harm our communities, such as the scourge of drugs, are of common concern. Emigration is of common concern, as we wish to see as many of our young people as possible make a life for themselves at home. Equality of opportunity must be available to everyone living on this island, irrespective of race, colour, gender, sexuality, disability, religion or politics. The securing of equality necessitates the creation of a powerful and effective culture of rights. Such rights would include the right to decent housing, in neighbourhoods free from the scourge of drugs, crime, poverty and unemployment; the right to vocational training and employment with a fair wage; the right to protection from hardship whether due to illness, disability, unemployment or old age; the right to legal protection from injustice and discrimination; the right to proper security; the right to live in freedom from violence, intimidation and fear; the right to education from nursery to third-level study and training; the right of everyone living on this island to think, vote, speak, read and worship as they please. Every citizen should have the right to freedom of information. The right to organise and campaign politically, whether in a trade union, political party or pressure group, should be guaranteed to all.

The above are representative of the rights that a real and committed application of the principle of equality would guarantee to all the people of Ireland. They are ideals whose time has come: inequality and coercion have failed in Ireland and it is time to take the logical steps to bring about change for the better. A society based upon equality for all remains the republican goal; its creation will be the realisation of the republican vision of an Ireland free from external interference and governed solely by the people of this island.

Finally I would like to share a quote from a contemporary Scottish writer and thinker, Tom Leonard, that I believe encapsulates the vision and brilliance of the United Irishmen in the language of today. 'Democracy is daily dialogue, and true democracy lies in the equality and the equal power of all parties to that dialogue.'

# 4

# The Concept of Republicanism

DES O'HAGAN

The concept of republicanism, as I understand it, has four distinct characteristics. It is in my view democratic, internationalist, secular and socialist. The absence of any of these features not only diminishes the global integrity of the concept but transforms it into a political philosophy hostile to the humanistic ethos that pervades the concept as analysed. The bloody murderous evidence for this is widespread.[1] This contribution will seek to elaborate these propositions and establish the critical importance of republicanism for the creation of a truly humane world in the new millennium. It will be obvious that the opinions expressed here, while personal in some senses, derive from the fact of my membership of the Workers' Party. In my view the Workers' Party, at this point in time, is the only authentic articulation of the republican tradition.

## A BRIEF REVIEW OF WORKERS' PARTY PHILOSOPHICAL DEVELOPMENT

The immediate origins of the Workers' Party lie in the period 1962–72. However the party in explaining its existence and nature traces its roots to the emergence of modern Ireland in around the late eighteenth century and the emergence, via Wolfe Tone and the United Irishmen, of the principles of the French Revolution – liberty, equality and fraternity – as the new, revolutionary dynamic in Irish political life. In its review of Irish history from that period the Workers' Party also stresses the progressive radical dimensions of popular republican struggle from Emmet, Lalor, Davitt, Connolly and Mellowes to the Republican Congress of the 1930s, as significant inputs into its present ideology.[2]

From roughly 1939 to 1962, the republican movement (Sinn Féin and the IRA) as a consequence of the War of Independence, partition and the outbreak of World War Two saw itself as having a single goal: the ending of partition and the creation of an 'independent' unitary state.[3] The only method whereby this could be achieved, it was believed, was a military campaign in Northern Ireland. (The bombing campaign in Britain in the 1940s was not repeated by the IRA in the 1956–62 campaign.) But by 1962 it was clear that the previous two decades had demonstrated not only the futility of 'military campaigns' but that the two states, Northern Ireland and the Republic, were now more firmly established than at any time since 1920.[4] Whilst romantic, heroic adventures might win short-term localised approval, they had no impact whatsoever on the politics of the two states; indeed if anything they were counterproductive, even in terms of the minimalist goal of an independent unified country.

From 1962, under the leadership of Cathal Goulding, the republican movement began a comprehensive review and philosophical historical analysis of modern Irish history and of the republican movement, its successes and failures.[5] Essentially this led to a rejection of militarism and the promotion of radical democratic politics in Northern Ireland and the Republic. Obviously the worldwide development of socialist revolutionary movements and anti-imperialist struggle helped to shape the new departure, as it became known.[6] Such a development was bound to generate organisational conflict and contradictions. However, unlike the Republican Congress period when the left walked away, Goulding and those who recognised and were actively involved in the politics of the radical evaluation stayed. Unfortunately the violent events surrounding the Northern Ireland Civil Rights Association campaign for a democratic Northern Ireland led to more severe contradictions and an opportunity for 'militant' narrow nationalistic elements to reinstate themselves as the 'real republican force'.

The formation of the Provisionals in 1970, dubbed by Sinn Féin at that time the Provisional Alliance, and subsequent serious terrorist and judicial violence delayed the politico-philosophical development of Sinn Féin.[7] (As others have noted, the curfew of the Lower Falls area of Belfast in July 1970, the introduction of internment in August 1971 and Bloody Sunday in Derry in January 1972 fuelled the violence and provided a 'justification' for the Provisional campaign. It has also been argued, reasonably, that British government strategy was to maximise violence in order to 'lance the boil'.)[8] Then, in May 1972, a prescient speech by party president Tomas Mac Giolla in Carrickmore, County Tyrone, renouncing terrorist sectarian violence and pointing out the inevitable tragic results, re-engaged the party with its internal philosophical struggle to build itself as a coherent, principled working-class political force in Irish politics.[9] That project was developed comprehensively throughout the following twenty years.

Elsewhere the Workers' Party has dealt in detail with the serious Democratic Left breakaway in 1992 led by the then president of the party Proinsias De Rossa.[10] It is important to state here that, as well as seeking to impose a dominant parliamentarianism, the De Rossa group abandoned core elements of party philosophy. As such it fits easily into the hostile category outlined in the opening paragraph of this chapter.

Somewhat like Tone himself, it was the historical experience of the party combined with ongoing internal education, discussion and reflection that brought the Workers' Party to the position where its ideology could be stated in the terms outlined in the first paragraph of this essay. In 1974, speaking at Bodenstown, Sean Garland spelled out the future direction the party would take.[11] But in no way should the ideological position of the Workers' Party be seen as a simple, uninterrupted linear progression from the 'nationalist militarism' of 1940–1960 to the coherent democratic socialist position of today. Apart from a number of violent assaults on the party itself, the ongoing sectarian, terrorist and fundamentalist situation has meant that the party has had to remain constantly vigilant to ensure adherence to its philosophy. Furthermore the political struggle to win broad support for that understanding has been conducted in the extremely hostile climate noted above. It has been distorted also by the general, possibly understandable though totally erroneous, perception of the term 'republican' as being synonymous with 'Roman Catholic' and 'nationalist'. At the same time it must be said that that perception has deliberately been encouraged in the media by both nationalists and unionists for their own purposes.

REPUBLICAN IMPERATIVES

To propose that adherence to any political philosophy imposes imperatives should neither be contentious nor startling. Equally to state that these imperatives must manifest themselves more or less coherently, ideologically, ethically, practically and theoretically, should be beyond disagreement.[12] To put this in the context of this essay demands, therefore, that there should be positive answers to the following questions: is there a republican ideology? or a republican ethic? or a republican practice? or a republican theory?[13] These answers in turn should provide a significant critique of Irish history, particularly over the past seventy years.

That these questions can be posed dispenses with what may be described as a minimalist republican understanding (namely, simple advocacy of a non-monarchical form of government) as totally inadequate. Although, obviously, it is logically impossible to conceive of a republic ruled even by what is now called a constitutional monarchy, at the same time the above point is critical to any serious politico-philosophical debate. Republican ideology was more than a critique of the *ancien régime*. At the same time it located the citizen at the centre of political discourse. Political institutions were no longer to be the playthings of a privileged aristocracy. This revolutionary concept of new democratic structures would progress on two levels: the extension of the franchise ultimately to include all citizens aged over eighteen years, and a deeper level which would manifest itself in the Paris Commune and soviets.

The clash between conflicting understandings,[14] between meaningful pervasive democratic politics and simple parliamentary representation, while no longer the burning issue it was between socialists and social democrats, is a core element in republican ideology. It is a debate which, while never seriously present in Irish politics, continued throughout Europe well into the twentieth century. That it is not currently a major point of ideological conflict owes more to the dramatic collapse of the socialist countries and the rise of gross individualism than it does to the merits of parliamentarianism. However the fact that republicanism is grounded in democratic understanding and places the citizen at the centre of political thought raises fundamental questions for all who protest their Irish republicanism.

That there are two states in Ireland, Northern Ireland and the Republic, is recognised by the vast majority in both societies. (There is a small minority who deny the validity of that claim; see note 4.) However on its own that statement, while valid, would be largely vacuous if it did not take into account the hostility of a significant proportion of nationalists to the northern state. The extreme point of view is expressed in the sentiment 'Northern Ireland is a failed entity – it is not reformable, it has to be dismantled totally'. The alternative, democratic view was expressed by republicans and became the inspiration of the Northern Ireland Civil Rights Association (NICRA), namely, one man, one vote.[15] In other words, NICRA located the citizen *qua* citizen at the centre of Northern Ireland political life; therefore it was a fundamental challenge to the sectarian institutions and social practices that had deformed the state.[16] The response of the then Unionist government to this challenge is sufficiently well known not to require further elaboration here. What is more significant is the fact that a whole series of progressive democratic reforms (political, economic and social) were triggered off by the civil rights movement on the one hand, while on the other the Provisionals began a terrorist campaign that has left a legacy of bitter sectarian division and hatred which will take generations to overcome.

In terms of republican ideology, therefore, the vicious Provisional sectarian terrorist campaign to supersede the civil-rights-inspired democratic struggle was objectively counter-revolutionary. A Roman Catholic nationalist ethic in fact became the driving force behind Provisionalism.[17] Obviously there are those who will dispute this vehemently, arguing that the Provisionals were motivated solely by the violent pursuit of 'national territorial unity' and an 'end to British rule in Ireland', demonstrably in keeping with the vision of Tone and the United Irishmen. However that claim cannot stand in isolation, as it is made as the virtual totality of the republican tradition. It would not only be crude reductionism to allow it to stand unscrutinised, it would denude republicanism of all that makes it a comprehensive, humane political philosophy.

CREATING MONSTERS

If it is correct to state, as has been claimed here, that republicanism places the citizen at the heart of its political philosophy, then the republican ethic must be congruent with that understanding. It will accord absolute primacy to the concept of 'citizen' as the form of political identification. Equally it will consider the pursuit of the maximisation of the citizen's interests, political, economic and social, as the highest good. In turn that ethic will dictate practice. It is just here, where ethics and practice coincide, that we can distinguish what can only be described as monster versions of republicanism.

Political ethics are ideals by which events, people, and movements are judged. Equally they set the parameters within which objectives and programmes are pursued. In the case of Irish republicanism the core ethical statement is Tone's refusal to submit to the tyranny of religious sectarianism; instead he proposes a secular model of a future independent Ireland.[18] Therefore it is incumbent on anyone who claims to be in the Tone tradition to recognise that their actions must be not only in keeping with their objectives but also subject to the ethical constraints of Tone's means. In other words, no matter how regular the pilgrimages to Bodenstown, or the ongoing ritualistic sloganising about 'the unity of Protestant, Catholic and Dissenter', republican authenticity and legitimacy must be judged on the contribution actions either make to securing Tone's 'means' or to frustrating them. Other forms of critical interpretation are important as will be apparent; nor should this be understood as dismissing 'external' criticisms of terrorist violence over the past thirty years. Indeed from any revolutionary standpoint, as pointed out already, objectively terrorist violence in Ireland has been counter-revolutionary. It should be only necessary then to show the type and range of vicious sectarian murders carried out by the Provisionals and the IRSP/INLA from 1970 to 1993 to demonstrate conclusively that they fit the monster version of republicanism.[19] The following stand out as particularly grotesque:

SEPTEMBER 1971, Four Step Inn, Shankill Road, bombed: 2 dead, 20 injured

DECEMBER 1971, Shankill Road furniture store, bombed: 4 dead (including 2 children)

MARCH 1972, Donegall Street, Belfast, bombed: 6 dead

JULY 1972, Bloody Friday, Belfast, 22 bombs killed 9, injured 130

JULY 1972, Claudy, County Derry, bombed: 9 killed

JUNE 1973, Coleraine, bombed: 6 killed, 18 injured

APRIL 1975, Mountainview Tavern, Shankill Road, bombed: 5 killed

AUGUST 1975, Bayardo Bar, Shankill Road, bombed: 5 killed and 40 injured

SEPTEMBER 1975, Orange hall, Newtownhamilton, machine-gunned: 4 killed

JANUARY 1976, Kingsmills, County Armagh: workers' bus machine-gunned: 10 killed

FEBRUARY 1978, La Mon Restaurant, near Belfast, bombed: 12 people burned to death, 30 injured

NOVEMBER 1983, Darkley Pentecostal Church, County Armagh: 3 elders shot dead

NOVEMBER 1987, Enniskillen, County Fermanagh, war memorial bombed: 11 dead, 63 injured

JANUARY 1992, Teebane, County Tyrone, workers' van bombed: 8 killed

OCTOBER 1993, Shankill Road, fish shop bombed: 9 killed (including 2 children).

(There were many other horrific murders of individual Protestants during these years; not to list them is not to imply that they were any less tragic for their grieving families nor that they lacked serious political implications.)

These heinous acts in turn demand that the organisations that carried out these murders be categorised in some manner other than as 'republicans'. It is not sufficient to dismiss them as simply 'murderous terrorist gangs'. The reality is that their persistence over time is evidence that they have gained a critical level of popular public support within the nationalist population and are therefore apparently 'acceptable', for whatever reasons, as an expression of that sector. Obviously this applies more to the

Provisionals than it does to the IRSP.[20]

Several serious questions, at different levels, arise from that understanding. It raises the issue of potential political convergence between Sinn Féin and the Social and Democratic Labour Party (SDLP) which has always been avowedly nationalist. Both parties draw their support almost exclusively from the Roman Catholic population, and as Sinn Féin increasingly has sought to project itself as the core of a dynamic new pan-nationalism, the process whereby Sinn Féin has sought to legitimise itself, inevitably therefore, has been couched in language, symbols and rituals entirely endogenous to the Roman Catholic nationalist people. It should be clear that this is a matter of absolute importance.

THE LEGITIMATION OF TERRORISM

The forms of legitimation, carried out strategically by the British, Irish and, notably, the American governments, are of a different order of significance. The admissions by the British government that it had had lengthy covert talks with the Provisionals, the creation of the Forum for Peace and Reconciliation by the Irish government, plus sympathetic noises in favour of a pan-nationalist front by Fianna Fáil, and the fulsome welcome accorded to Sinn Féin leaders at different times in Washington, in addition to the Clinton visit to Northern Ireland, were all directed at absorbing Sinn Féin into the 'constitutional process'. This is not to attribute common motivation to the three governments, but they did have that purpose in common. In so doing they also accelerated and reinforced the process of legitimation within the Roman Catholic nationalist people. But by virtue of that, they have contributed substantially to intensifying notions of 'separate development' in Northern Ireland, a concept which obviously is implacably hostile to the republican ethics of citizenship and democracy, as well as, one imagines, not being particularly supportive of the peace process. Sinn Féin, not simply for tactical electoral reasons, as some might wish to have it, has cooperated fully in this process of 'separate nationalist development'. The plethora of 'community organisations' in nationalist areas funded, directly or indirectly, by the Northern Ireland Office and founded by or closely associated with Sinn Féin is sufficient evidence to justify this statement, although there are other equally strong arguments.

In effect, therefore, the location of Sinn Féin within the political domain designated by the combination of the three concepts identified here (political convergence, endogenous legitimation and separate development), reinforced by their 'freedom struggle', invalidates any claims whatsoever it might make to being within the republican tradition and places it firmly within sectarian Roman Catholic nationalism. Moreover, the fact that this analysis has proceeded latterly by seeking to understand and engage with the interpretations that Sinn Féin itself employs avoids the risk, and possible accusation, of 'becoming vacuous and circular'.[21]

There is one final point to be made at this time. It concerns the process whereby Sinn Féin has legitimised itself within the Roman Catholic community while at the same time insisting that it is a republican organisation. There are three possible different critical interpretations of that position: (1) the charitable, (2) the rigorous republican, and (3) the 'discontented' acceptance of incoherence. (The latter is interesting sociologically in the light of the apparent transfer of voting preference within the nationalist community from the SDLP to Sinn Féin. In West Belfast the transfer is a notional 9.75 per cent.) First, however, it is necessary to explicate further the modes of legitimation in terms of language, symbols and rituals. Although these concepts overlap in various ways (for example, language as symbol, or ritual as symbol) it should be profitable to analyse them separately.

The use of language for legitimation is understood here to operate on three levels: the coded, the explicit and the exclusive (that is, the Provisionalisation of Gaelic). Over the years the constant reiteration of 'Brits out' has come to be understood within the nationalist population as applying to anyone identified as British. This serves the dual purpose of reinforcing the Roman

Catholic population's sense of 'Irishness' and at the same time intimates that the Protestant population should be expelled, without resorting to explicit threats. *In no way should this be extended to mean that the Roman Catholic population concur with this threat.* In the explicit use of language it has become more than noticeable that the Provisional leadership has constantly interchanged the concepts of 'Catholic', 'nationalist' and 'republican', quite often within the one speech or press release. The intention is obvious.

As the Irish language in Northern Ireland has tended to be taught virtually entirely within Roman Catholic schools, it is no wonder that Sinn Féin has found it easy to usurp the language's cultural–linguistic functions and recruit it to its legitimation process: Gaelic as an exclusive means of 'national self-identification' and also as a sectarian instrument to designate 'the outsider'. (The deliberate speaking of Irish in council chambers where it is absolutely clear that the speaker will not be understood is a classic example.)

Symbols may be interpreted relatively autonomously or as highly significant interactive justificatory components of ritual: for example, the flying of flags or the wearing of emblems. Social context is obviously critical to both situations. A flag above a government building is it own justification; a flag waved in front of a demonstration may well provoke violence. In intermediary situations – the flying of the Irish tricolour in parts of west Belfast, for example – the flag serves to reinforce separateness and inform 'the outsider' of that fact: we are Irish, you are not!

Of even greater interest are wall murals as symbols. In particular we should note those that deal with subjects in a quasi-religious fashion: for example, the mural of the emaciated Christ-like hunger striker fingering a set of rosary beads or the Irish Famine depicted as identical to the holocaust suffered by the Jews under Nazism. As religion plays a critical role in mediating and imposing concepts, it is clear here that there is, on the one hand, an appeal to religion to justify and sanctify individual 'sacrifice' and on the other, the claim that it was because of their religion that the Irish were 'sacrificial' victims of a holocaust/famine. Once again, the purpose is to intensify solidarity within the Roman Catholic population by emphasising, historically and currently, *their* 'suffering' and *their* 'sacrifice' and at the same time to assert the almost sacred nature of Sinn Féin as a component of these 'sacrifices'. The fact that these images could reasonably be described as blasphemous and that this has gone unchallenged is a strong index of the extent to which Sinn Féin has been legitimised within the Roman Catholic population.

Rituals abound in both political and civil society; being commonplace, they tend not to be subject to critical scrutiny, unless they are, or become, absurd, redundant or counterproductive. Rituals may be divided into two categories: the sacred and the profane, although the boundaries are often blurred. For example the playing of the English Roman Catholic hymn 'Faith of Our Fathers', a celebration of martyrdom and imprisonment, as a pre-match ritual at GAA All-Ireland Finals (now discontinued) certainly suggested at least, if in a confused way, that Gaelic football was a Roman Catholic sport.

It was undoubtedly during the 1981 hunger strike period that the most impressive Provisional symbolism and ritual emerged. The proliferation of black flags, the marches, demonstrations, meetings, religious ceremonies, funerals and massive national and international media coverage penetrated deep into the consciousness of the nationalist population and provided a comprehensive social base among Roman Catholic voters for the future political growth of Sinn Féin. It would be difficult to overestimate the impact of this period. Ritual, tricolour-draped coffins, guards of honour, sombre cortèges played a major part in imprinting the individual 'sacrifice' on even the non-participating nationalist population. While there was criticism of the entire hunger strike scenario, for example from the Workers' Party, nationalist Ireland identified with the tide of sentiment released during this period.

## SINN FÉIN – THE NEW NATIONALISM?

My critique of the process of legitimation undertaken by Sinn Féin, as outlined so far, comes under what has been described as 'rigorous republicanism'. This position has seldom been aired in the mass media.[22] In fact because its main, if not only, proponent is the Workers' Party it has been treated as an in-house squabble, when examined at all. A significant part of the reason for this, as far as some journalists in the nationalist media are concerned, is the desire to avoid any accusations of being pro-unionist; others have active sympathy for the Provisional position. Even where there is a feeling of unease or revulsion, the argument takes the form: 'Yes, these acts cannot be condoned, but...' In reality this is equivalent to stating that the ultimate responsibility for whatever terrorist crime is under discussion lies not with the perpetrators but elsewhere. Hence this interpretation has been designated 'charitable'. It could equally be described as tribal or ethnocentric.

The significant electoral gains made by Sinn Féin since 1983 can be attributed to a number of factors. There is no doubt that the hunger strike period, as already pointed out, provided a mass social base within the Roman Catholic community for this development. However, as the SDLP overall percentage vote has remained constant, it would seem that Sinn Féin has attracted both significant numbers of first- or second-time voters and, at the same time, in some areas, voters previously committed to the SDLP. Although there is no hard information to confirm this, many commentators feel that a critical part of this Sinn Féin vote represents a new Roman Catholic middle class extremely conscious of its lack of political power in Northern Ireland. They have benefited from third-level education and are now in professional occupations or are potentially socially mobile. Overall they are discontented with a society that does not enshrine their cultural values. At the same time they have identified Sinn Féin as the modern political vehicle[23] most likely to meet their aspirations, not in terms of its supposed republicanism, but because of its deliberate incoherence, that is, the mixing of 'Catholic', 'nationalist' and 'republican'. It is reasonable also to assume that they appreciate current changes in the demographic structure of Northern Ireland and the Republic, both denominational and class. Questions of minority and majority therefore are being reinvented in terms of the 'new' nationalism which its supporters see Sinn Féin as representing. It is absolutely and unapologetically Roman Catholic but it also reflects the triumphalist middle-class consciousness that is a result of the Republic's 'tiger economy' and the social mobility noted above. There is a sense also, a feeling, a belief, that the world of Northern Ireland is their creation, or at least that they have been significantly instrumental as midwives at its birth. Their reality can only be understood, then, in strictly Hegelian terms, as they are either ignorant or scornful of legislation, from the key 1947 Education Act to anti-discrimination laws which are the direct consequence of post-war socialist conviction and the civil rights movement. Obviously there is nothing really new in this nationalism.[24]

REPUBLICANISM AS A CRITIQUE OF NATIONALISM

It is not possible here to provide a comprehensive republican ideological critique of nationalism, but two obvious dimensions require exploration concerning republicanism: (1) specifically as the most formidable opponent of Irish nationalism and (2) at the more general level of political thought. The concept of republicanism, as understood by the Workers' Party, while it is shaped by critical aspects of Irish historical experience, is no mere expression of that experience. Consequently there will be considerable overlap between these two sections.

In relation to the first dimension, a brief account of the Workers' Party programme should illustrate beyond question the manner in which it contradicts both constitutional and violent Irish nationalism. The ultimate goal of the Workers' Party is the creation of a democratic secular, socialist, unitary state on the island of Ireland – a republic. In 1985 the party stated,

'To achieve this objective The Workers' Party will have won the support of the overwhelming majority of the working class in Northern Ireland and the Republic of Ireland. It cannot be achieved by coercion or subterfuge.' We also said, 'the existence of two States North and South is a reality and they cannot be bombed out of existence or wished out of existence.' And in defence of democracy and democratic institutions, we declared;

> It does no good at this time, no matter how true, to point out that the history of opposition in Northern Ireland, to say the least of it, was absolutely impoverished, for it could be equally levelled that the quality of government in Northern Ireland until after 1945 bordered on the reactionary grotesque.
>
> Our concern, therefore, must be to rescue the principle of democratic government and establish effective, responsible, humane, far-seeing and courageous institutions.

Later we stated what we believed to be the most pressing needs of the time:

> Our immediate concern must be to develop democratic politics in Northern Ireland, end terrorism and bring about the complete demilitarisation of our society.... We are opposed to direct rule because it denies democracy; we reject sectarian solutions because they are anti-political, we seek democratic political solutions.[25]

The Workers' Party's international activity also demonstrates conclusively its commitment to democratic, peaceful, egalitarian, libertarian principles in opposition to the history of the nationalist parties toadying to various American administrations. That international activity stretches back to support for the democratically elected Marxist government in Chile of President Salvador Allende, brutally murdered and overthrown by a CIA-controlled terrorist *coup*, and to the party's ongoing and present support of the Cuban people against the illegal American embargo.

> Internationalism, then, for The Workers' Party is not an afterthought. Naturally therefore as we built the Party into

> Ireland's first modern socialist party we established friendly relations with many parties, movements, organisations and states in different parts of the world. We identified key criteria – that they shared our views on democracy, socialism, world peace and disarmament, democratic political struggle and opposition to terrorism.
>
> Let us give some examples. We supported the Vietnamese people in their struggle against the barbarous American imperialist aggression; we provided medical aid to the MPLA Workers' Party of Angola and we have constantly supported the African National Congress in their opposition to Apartheid and the racialist South African regime; we have had as guests at our Annual Ard Fheis representatives from the Palestinian Liberation Organisation, Cuba, China, Korea, the former USSR and the GDR and various parties and groups of parties from the Japanese Communist Party to the Left Unity Group in the European Parliament.
>
> Not least among our international activity was the promotion of the European Committee for Peace and Security which emerged from the 1975 Helsinki Final Act. Indeed The Workers' Party through the Irish Committee did more than any of our native governments to promote understanding among our people of the contribution which the ECSC process was making to preserve peace and understanding during the difficult years of division in Europe.
>
> While clearly all these activities and associations placed us firmly on the side [of] and within the 'socialist camp' the Party at all times preserved its independence and integrity in dealing with all our foreign comrades.[26]

It should be obvious even from these short selections from Workers' Party publications that they are imbued with a political understanding firmly embedded in a political philosophy that prioritises democracy and democratic struggle, egalitarian international human relations, opposition to warmongering and imperialist domination, and above all identification with the oppressed and exploited peoples of the world. In brief they are the modern expression of 'liberty, equality and fraternity'. It should be unnecessary to contrast this in detail with the national and international programmes of Fianna Fáil and the Provisionals. In terms of Irish politics, sufficient has been written already to locate them outside the republican tradition.

However it is important to note the ongoing erosion of Irish neutrality and equally the intensification of the linkages between the Provisionals and the American administration. While there are significant vestiges of Irish neutrality which enable the Republic to play an important role in relation to non-aligned countries, it is clear that there is no republican concept of identification with the exploited rather than the exploiters. Furthermore it would appear that the present Fianna Fáil government has opened the door via the Amsterdam Treaty to full Irish military integration into NATO (likewise agreed to by the previous coalition) and to the total surrender of relatively independent decision-making as regards foreign policy.

As for the Povisionals, over the years they have been identified with right-wing Irish American organisations and opinion. Now apparently they have the support and encouragement of the highly suspect and sinister American National Endowment for Democracy and its subsidiary the National Democratic Institute. This is hardly surprising, given the connection that existed between key Noraid figures and the CIA in the mid-seventies, and the manner in which Noraid's New York newspaper the *Irish People* headlined their murders and shooting of members and supporters of the Workers' Party: 'Provisional wedge against communism in Ireland' (November 1975).

In terms of our second dimension of republicanism's critique of nationalism, at the level of political thought, at one level it is possible to be comfortable with the concept of nationalism. It offers an easily understood answer to the question 'Who are you?' – Irish, German, French, American, English, Russian or whatever. Within this mode of identification one can also detect other nonthreatening senses, for example, matters of language, history, culture, which project a feeling of specific belonging or the very human emotion of love of home. And even though this everyday concept of nationalism can be harshly competitive, as in the Olympic Games or the World Cup, it is very much a modern part of the human condition and contributes significantly to the wide, colourful and variegated nature of humankind. Without these differences the world would undoubtedly be a poorer place.

However, it is not at this mundane, 'family rivalry' level that republicanism confronts and opposes nationalism and its associated concepts. Rather it is nationalism as the proximate cause of the slaughter of billions over the past two centuries; it is nationalism as the cornerstone of the vicious racialism expressed in Nazism and Fascism, in the equally vicious system of South African apartheid, and in the grotesque posturing and violence of the Ku Klux Klan, the National Front and the vociferous neo-Nazi organisations that pollute a growing number of states in Europe; it is the nationalism of 'blood and soil' which republicanism abhors as a dangerous and evil phenomenon. It is nationalist expansionism, 'Trade follows the flag', which was the enabling sentiment for the development of imperialism and the consequent enslavement of millions. It is important then to recognise that there is absolutely no difference between any of the modern imperialisms, British, German, French, American and Japanese, a fact that seems to have escaped the notice of many Irish nationalists.

Obviously nationalism was a necessary but not sufficient condition for the emergence of imperialism. But having played that part it has ceased to be significant in world politics in the sense in which it engaged political thought for more than two centuries. The key issues of national sovereignty and national self-determination have become redundant since the end of World War Two, for at least three reasons: the discovery and use of atomic energy in the military sphere; the role of international monopoly capitalism and the multinationals; and the global imperialist hegemony of the United States of America. This is not to say that the world has been inoculated against the 'virus of nationalism'. On the contrary it continues to be the cause of serious and violent confrontations in the service of those who elevate the idea of the nation to 'something mystical, intangible and supernatural'.[27] At a deeper level of significance this nationalist metaphysic, as pointed out earlier, by demanding that its 'sacred' character be recognised and accepted, seeks to establish its moral authority and supremacy over republicanism – a profane, concrete and human construct. Having overthrown and defeated the 'divine right of kings' the republic faces a more sinister challenge in as much as its appeal is not to the priestly laying on of hands and anointing with blessed oil, but to a concept that recognises no higher authority than itself. Taken to its extreme the implications are clear. Argument, dialogue, rationality, politics, even morality are inevitably sidelined. Any action, no matter how obscene, can be justified by asserting that it is in the interest of the nation. That this has been and is the case, particularly in this century, cannot be gainsaid.

There is, therefore, clearcut political confrontation between republican values, as outlined here, and demonic nationalism and global capitalism. The development of that conflict will be conducted on local, regional and international fronts. Central to it must be the concept of free, equal, responsible citizenship. We can assume no more than this in any dialogue that may develop. Indeed, some will argue that it is widely optimistic to imagine such an initial consensus, others that it is too minimalist to be of any real value. To accept either of these views would be a denial of hope. Equally it would be to surrender to a darker side of humanity which thrives, in Auden's words, on 'hate for hate's sake' or asserts the primacy of individual greed as the fundamental good. Our world is experiencing the grotesque consequences of these evils; it is more than time then, again in Auden's words, 'to fight back with such courage as you have' guided by political, economic and moral principles that articulate the vision encapsulated in the slogan 'liberty, equality and fraternity'.

## CONCLUSION

One of the immediate results of the virtual worldwide comprehensive triumph of capitalism led by the USA and of the total collapse of the European socialist states has been the conclusion that no real ideological challenge can be mounted to capitalism's hegemony.[28] Many have echoed the celebrated anti-communist Vaclav Havel, now president of the Czech Republic, who proclaimed, 'socialism is dead'. This proclamation had been taken up by various shades of social democrats but most significantly by the American radical intellectual J.K. Galbraith. In a lecture delivered in Britain he called for 'constructive pragmatism' and stated, 'In dealing with the economic system we can no longer believe that there are controlling principles – socialist principles, social democratic principles, in the United States liberal principles.'[29] In short, he added, 'We are for what works best.' This is elaborated in two unambiguous statements: 'Our claim is not to violent change, certainly not to revolution. It is to a socially better performance by the existing system.'

The modernisers of the British Labour Party took up Galbraith's thesis with gusto. Roy Hattersley, for example, in an article in the London *Times* (23 February 1993) stated that 'slogans about nationalisation were an alternative to thought'; he advocated the dropping of the British Labour Party's commitment to nationalisation (state ownership of the means of production, distribution and exchange) contained in Clause 4 of its constitution and its replacement with R.H. Tawney's famous statement 'Socialism is the gospel of freedom – the utmost development of every human being and *the deliberate organisation of society for the attainment of that objective*' (emphasis added). Unfortunately Hattersley did not examine the implications of Tawney's dictum or he could hardly have advocated the abject surrender of state-owned public companies to rapacious finance capital. And clearly, whatever else motivates it, the Blair government's agenda is not being directed by Tawney's vision. It is ironic that some of the early 'modernisers' are now calling for a halt to the Labour government's sordid romance with free market liberalism. In Ireland the Democratic Left enthusiastically welcomed the advice of Professor Fred Halliday of the London School of Economics: 'The best we can go for is a radical interpretation of what capitalist democracy has to offer' (*Irish Times*, 4 July 1993).

It is reasonable to suggest that these two examples of the jettisoning of socialist ideology are indicative of a European (if not worldwide) malaise of political spirit which derives from a despairing sentiment that socialism can no longer confront and defeat capitalism, from a realisation that expanding religious fundamentalism and nationalism are threatening even bourgeois democracy, and from the corrosive 'market' individualism that is modern liberalism. As a result of this malaise there is now a somewhat frantic casting about for an alternative public philosophy. It could be argued that the concept of republicanism as outlined here would meet that need. (But see note 13. The advent of socialist understanding certainly depended politically on the republican concepts, but socialist states, no matter what their later defects in practice, transcended any contemporary republic.) However it is obvious that this concept of republicanism would require an explosive revolution in political thought and popular understanding even greater and more widespread than that which preceded the October Revolution in 1917. At this point in time it is difficult to see this taking place, given the ideological and military hegemony of international monopoly capitalism, though it would be wrong to come to facile conclusions about the end of politics.[30]

It is not just simply that the private ownership of all the means of material production is assured under capitalism: privatisation actually destroys the foundations upon which the democratic state and society supposedly rests – resulting in private ownership of mass communications, of political parties (consider the role of funding) and of critical educational institutes. Increasingly not only is the democratic deficit growing, but the alienation of a massive section of the citizenry is the norm. The concept of democracy therefore is one field where a campaign for real and extensive change could be initiated; if developed nationally and internationally, a campaign could set in motion powerful forces promoting the other values inherent in republican ideology.

Who will undertake this and how it is to be done are vital questions which need to be addressed now. It would be our opinion that within the European Union, at least, all the serious socialist, workers', communist and other broad popular democratic forces must contribute to the revitalisation of the ideological struggle.[31] The fightback has begun, to some extent, in different countries and at different levels. But as capitalism develops its common European mansion with strategic headquarters in Brussels and Strasbourg, the urgency of our concern to begin building a common European home within which the citizen will be lord and master is clear. It demands a new unity of thought, of purpose and of action. It can draw on the strengths (and mistakes) of the past; it demands, also, that we create a leadership with a bright and inspiring vision of a world unified in the pursuit of human freedom.

## NOTES

1 The eruption over the past twenty years alone of violent religious and nationalist fundamentalism has led to atrocities on a widespread scale comparable to the barbarism of the Nazis in the towns and villages of Eastern Europe during World War Two. The terrorist militants involved now often propagandise themselves as 'republicans'. Croatian and Islamic fundamentalists are probably the two most notorious examples.

2 See George Gilmore, *The Republican Congress* (Cork: Cork Workers' Club, 1974). Unfortunately, key left-wing figures, Gilmore, O'Donnell, Ryan and Price among others, walked away from the republican movement. This disastrous decision shaped the political orientation of the movement for almost thirty years. Many Republican Congress supporters were to fight and die for the Spanish Republic against Franco's Fascism.

3 The republican movement was the generic title for Sinn Féin and the IRA. The latter was the dominant force, headed by the Army Council. In reality this meant that politics of any kind was absolutely subordinate to militarism, until the emergence of Cathal Goulding. In a recent conversation Goulding insisted that the Army Executive played a major part in the transformation. However, this should not be understood, in my opinion, as diminishing Goulding's critical contribution. Crucial dates in the development of the Workers' Party were: 1969–70, when the Provisionals left because of the then Sinn Féin's decision to take seats in Dáil Eireann (the southern parliament) if successful in any future elections; 1975, when the Seamus Costello faction (subsequently known as the Irish National Liberation Army) was expelled for seeking to reverse the party's anti-terrorist and pro-democracy stance on Northern Ireland; and 1977, when the suffix 'the Workers' Party' was added to the party name Sinn Féin, indicating the progressive political development of the party. In 1982 the party became known simply as the Workers' Party.

4 Both states in Ireland were considered to be illegal by the republican movement as they were created by the diktat of Britain. Legal political authority was held by the IRA Army Council as the inheritors of the mantle of the first Dáil of 1919. The Provisionals now seem to have abandoned this position and it appears to have been taken up by Republican Sinn Féin and the Continuity IRA.

5 A lifelong republican from a strongly left-wing family, Goulding when he became leader of the republican movement set about reorganisation with a clear detemination to prioritise democratic socialist politics.

Goulding was the first Marxist to hold this position.
6 For a period the term 'new departure' was avoided as its opponents argued that it implied an abandonment of the republican tradition.
7 The name Provisional Alliance was a reasonably accurate description of the group headed by Seán Mac Stiofáin. Key figures in Fianna Fáil, right-wing Irish Americans, ex-members of the IRA from the 1940s, Roman Catholic nationalists and ultra-left elements combined to create the Provisional Alliance.
8 See for example Dr Maurice Hayes, *Minority Verdict* (Belfast: Blackstaff Press, 1995) and his report of a conversation with Sir John Anderson, first commander-in-chief of the Ulster Defence Regiment.
9 Cllr Tomas Mac Giolla was president of the Workers' Party from 1962 to 1988. He was elected to Dublin Corporation in 1979 and became Lord Mayor in 1993/94. Elected to the Dáil in 1982, he was the only TD to remain loyal to the Workers' Party in 1992.
10 See *Patterns of Betrayal – the Flight from Socialism* (Dublin: Repsol, 1992). It contains all published contributions both by the Workers' Party and by spokespersons for the breakaway group in the run-up to the special ard fheis (annual delegate conference) of 1992.
11 Sean Garland was general secretary of the Workers' Party from 1977 to 1991. Currently he is party treasurer. His speech at Bodenstown, drawing on the insights of V.I. Lenin, stressed the necessity to create a revolutionary vanguard party.
12 See C. Wright Mills, *The Marxists* (Harmondsworth: Penguin, 1963). This formulation is taken entirely from Mills.
13 It could be argued quite reasonably that the ontological status of the concept of socialism, that is the comprehensive nature of its domain, subsumes the other three republican categories outlined here.
14 See Edmund Burke's 'Address to the Electors of Bristol' of 3 November, 1774, after his election. Burke saw himself as a representative and not a delegate. He rejected '*authoritative* instructions, *mandates* issued, which a member is bound blindly and implicitly to obey, to vote, and to argue for ... [which] arise from a fundamental mistake of the whole order and tenor of our constitution'. See *Edmund Burke*, edited by Isaac Kramnick (New Jersey, 1974). A similar type of argument was employed by De Rossa and his associates in 1992, though their emphasis was on not being bound by the party leadership and the decisions of the party ard fheis.
15 The Northern Ireland civil rights movement was understood by the Unionist government to be a plot to overthrow the state and bring about a 'united Ireland'. See the speech by the Minister for Home Affairs, William Craig, at the Ulster Hall, Belfast, on 28 November 1968. Other

Unionist MPs would later echo that sentiment.

16 This very much in keeping with Tone's 1793 comment on the state of catholics at the time: 'if they were to rise, and, with one voice, demand their rights as *citizens* and as men?' (emphasis added). See Sean Cronin, *For Whom the Hangman's Noose Was Spun* (Dublin: Repsol, 1991), a short but very valuable account of Tone and the United Irishmen.

17 In a very real sense this made it easy for Fianna Fáil elements and Irish Americans to throw their considerable weight behind the Provisionals. As Victor Griffin, former Dean of St Patrick's Cathedral, Dublin, points out in his illuminating autobiography *Mark of Protest* (Dublin: Gill and Macmillan, 1993): 'And in politics too we were seen as outsiders, not truly Irish, in the nation but not of it. To be Irish meant being Roman Catholic, Nationalist, Gaelic and anti-British.' This is a fairly acute description of Fianna Fáil philosophy but a far cry from republicanism. Some may feel that this cannot be substantiated, but the recent presidential decision by Fianna Fáil would seem to bear this criticism out. See also the *Irish Times*, 24 October 1997. Columnist Fintan O'Toole, referring to the Fianna Fáil candidate as 'in many ways typical of the Northern Catholic middle-class', goes on to ask, 'Doesn't Fianna Fáil deserve credit for the fact that, for once, they have lived up to their own rhetoric and put forward an outstandingly articulate and able representative of the kind of Ireland they aspire to?'

18 Tone asserted, 'To unite the whole people of Ireland, to abolish the memory of all past dissensions, and to substitute the common name of Irishman, in place of the denominations of Protestant, Catholic and Dissenter – these were my means' (1793). It is essential to note in this context that the *means* referred to by Tone relate to his *objects*: 'to assert the independence of my country'. Marianne Elliott in her definitive biography *Wolfe Tone: Prophet of Irish Independence* (Yale University Press, 1989) makes a similar point: 'His [Tone's] central message was not that Ireland's abiding evil was England, but rather that her people were disunited. Resolve the one and the other would resolve itself naturally.' One either accepts the primacy of Tone's understanding of citizenship and its implications for republicanism or else dismisses it as so much arrant nonsense.

19 This is in no way to ignore the heinous murder campaigns carried out over the years by various loyalist terrorist organisations and their brutal impact on the Roman Catholic community. The Provisionals seized the opportunity to present themselves as the defenders of the Roman Catholic community by murdering Protestants. The obvious historical comparison is with the Defenders and Peep o' Day Boys of Tone's era.

20 There has been consistent support for Sinn Féin in Northern Ireland from 1983 when they won 13.4 per cent of the overall vote in the general election, to the election of Adams (West Belfast) and McGuinness (Mid-Ulster) to Westminster in May 1997. Sinn Féin won over 40 per cent of the nationalist vote in that election. There are very real problems in interpreting this. It is ludicrous to dismiss their voters as 'delinquent' as has one journalist. Their vote can be understood in a benign fashion as a vote for peace; alternatively it may be seen as a conscious endorsement of the brutal sectarian nationalism espoused by Sinn Féin. (See also below.)

21 'Concepts and Society' in Dorothy Emmet and Alasdair MacIntyre (eds.), *Social Theory and Philosophical Analysis* (Macmillan, 1970). Gellner also argues, 'There must, one hopes, be some middle way, which allows interpretation, which allows some but not all of the context to be incorporated into the meaning of the concept, thus avoiding an unrealistic literal-minded scholasticism, and also escaping circularity of explanation. The problem concerns the rules and limits of invocation of social *context* in interpreting the participants' concepts.' But murderous acts such as La Mon, Loughinisland and Luxor transcend their social context. They are intrinsically evil and require no further description whatever in explanation. The remaining part of this section draws heavily on Gellner's criticisms of social anthropological interpretation.

22 An exception to this was a letter by F. Donnelly published in the *Mid Ulster Mail* (14 August 1997). In part it said, 'The creation of the Provisional Alliance in 1969 by elements within Fianna Fáil, aided by northern accomplices, was the greatest disaster to hit Ireland since the formation of the Orange Order in 1795. Both were reactionary forces and both had retrograde effects on the situation in Northern Ireland. Both were spawned with the intention of crushing genuine republican ideals and of halting the growing solidarity among people of all creeds in pursuit of their common interests.'

23 The jocose transformation of 'Tiochfaidh ar la' (Our day will come) into 'Tiochfaidh Armani' is possibly more telling than any survey of social attitudes would be.

24 It is worth noting in this context that the history of Fianna Fáil (the self-declaimed Republican Party) suggests that there is little to choose between the essentials of their platform and the Provisionals: both seek a nationalist solution to the Irish question; they identify the majority in sectarian terms and both reduced republican ideology to spurious separatism. To what extent Fianna Fáil could ever have been considered a serious republican party is a moot question; certainly it has changed or has been changed since the de Valera era. But it may be that this is more in

appearance than in real substance. The overt sectarianism of the 1937 Constitution has gone, in particular the special position accorded the Roman Catholic Church, the denial of divorce and contraceptive rights which derived from that position. Now it would certainly be considered a serious gaff in Upper Mount Street to echo de Valera's 'Labour must wait' or to reassert his pledge of the Irish people's allegiance to the Papacy. While the rural-led closed-society populism of de Valera's Fianna Fáil has been displaced to some extent by the opening up of the South to international capitalism under Lemass, the value system, as pointed out already, has remained the same. The most potent symbol of this fact was the choice of Mary McAleese by Fianna Fáil for the 1997 presidential election. Whatever about the new president's own value system, it cannot be denied that she is perceived as representing the Roman Catholic nationalistic ethos. This perception is based on the fact that, among other things, McAleese represented the Irish Roman Catholic hierarchy at the New Ireland Forum in 1983.

25 See *The Case for Devolved Government in Northern Ireland* (Dublin: Repsol, 1985). See also *Manifesto for the Millennium* (Dublin: Workers' Party, 1997) for a brief account of the Workers' Party's history and political perspectives.

26 *The Future Is Socialism* (Dublin: Workers' Party, November, 1993).

27 Joseph Stalin, *Marxism and the National and Colonial Question* (London, Martin Lawrence Limited). Much of what Stalin wrote in 1913 might now be considered largely of academic interest. There are, however, striking comments on the class implications of 'inciting nations against each other' which startle with their modernity. The pogrom had been replaced by ethnic cleansing in the obscene language of the 'new' nationalists. It seems little has changed at certain levels.

28 The extent, financing, planning and depth of the American assault on socialist ideology is conveyed in a lecture, 'Waging the War of Ideas: Why There Are No Short Cuts', delivered by John Blundell, President of the Institute of Economic Affairs, to the Heritage Foundation (July 1990). He identifies F.A. Hayek's *Road to Serfdom* (March, 1944) – a powerful attack on socialism and an eloquent plea for a liberal market order as the intellectual source which enabled the funding of a series of reactionary foundations, in the USA and Britain, and the purchase of intellectuals in every field. Among those who appreciated the contribution of the British Institute of Economic Affairs was Mrs Thatcher. After her election in 1979 she said, 'You created the atmosphere which made our victory possible.' It is interesting to note also that Milton Friedman (author of *Capitalism and Freedom*), the Chicago monetarist who had links with the

overthrow of Allende, is mentioned as a leading acolyte of Hayek. This astonishingly frank lecture should be read by all who believe that the present victory of capitalism can be overturned. I am indebted to Sean Garland for drawing my attention to this lecture.

29 For a more detailed look at Galbraith's arguments and associated viewpoints put forward around the same time see *The Future is Socialism* (Dublin: Workers' Party, November 1993).

30 Martin Jacques, former editor of *Marxism Today*, writing in the *Sunday Times* (July 1993) proclaimed 'the end of politics'. He argued that 'there is throughout the democratic world, a turn away from ideology towards pragmatism'.

31 'The Soviet experiment was only one of various conceivable experiments, and its failure does not impeach the possibility of more successful attempts' (J. Roemer, *A Future for Socialism*, London: Verso, 1994). Quoted in 'Analytical and Essential Marxism', Alan Carling (*Political Studies*, 1997 vol. XLV). A number of things could be said about this statement; in particular it does not mean that its opposite is true, namely that capitalism is successful. It also does not take into account Soviet successes in education, health and employment, three key areas in any economy. I am indebted to Ultan Gillen for drawing my attention to this article and for other valuable research assistance.

# 5

# Reclaiming Republicanism

EAMON HANNA

What matters is myth, not in the sense of fiction, but in the construction of a past elaborated by a political community for its own ends.

ROBERT GILDEA

1798, SOCIAL DEMOCRACY AND NORTHERN NATIONALISM

The seven-year history of the United Irish movement and the events of 1798 have never passed into history because they have never left the realm of contemporary political discourse. As I write, we are at a time, I hope, when all traditions in Ireland are at the foothills of a trek to the summit of a comprehensive political settlement. In the bicentenary year we can revisit the events of 1798, reflect on them, learn their lessons. Perhaps also we can let those events pass into history, and move on.

In the North of Ireland, groups from right across the political spectrum, from the Orange Order to Sinn Féin, have announced plans to mark 1798. It is remarkable that there is still a sufficient sense of shared history for 1798 to be noted in this way. It never happened in 1898 or 1948. It has never happened with any of the other significant dates of Irish history such as 1641, 1690, 1801 or 1916.

Unionism and nationalism are the two significant sources of political identity in modern Ireland. For anyone who draws even part of their consciousness or political literacy from those sources, myth and reality can present both opportunities and challenges. What happened in 1798 should now be at a sufficient distance to allow a dispassionate examination of the chain of events that, within seven years of the foundation of the first Society of United Irishmen in Belfast in October 1791, ended by the summer of 1798 in the most intense period of bloodshed in Irish history, with 30,000 dead in a matter of weeks.

An eminent Irish historian has observed that it is dangerous and unwise to read Irish history backwards. A modern English interloper into our politics (Enoch Powell) once noted that, in the North, 'sincerity is an overrated virtue'. Yet even after stripping back the encrustations of myth and distortion, it is still possible to justify the view that the brief years of the United Irish movement saw the creation of the first vision of a non-sectarian, democratic and inclusive politics which could sustain and nurture all the people of Ireland in their inherited complexity.

What thinkers like Tone borrowed from the American and French revolutions was the idea, new to Ireland, that Irish society could be structured with authority flowing from the bottom up rather than the top down. Not only that, but the United Irishmen saw the existing religious, ethnic and political diversity of Ireland as an opportunity rather than a problem and as a chance to create a shared future. The United Irish vision represents a brief break in the heavy cloud cover of Ascendancy, majoritarianism, the politics of the safety of numbers and the idea that the winner takes all. It was a brief, shining moment of possibility before tribal loyalties were set in concrete.

It should be possible to view the events of 1798 in something of a flame-proof environment, a benefit which was denied to the participants of the time. The model for us should be the élan and subtlety with which in 1989 the French marked the bicentenary of the French Revolution.

There is a scene in Wilde's comedy of manners *The Importance of Being Earnest* where Miss Prism, a middle-aged, blue-stocking tutor, warns her pupil, and the play's heroine, the somewhat frivolous Gwendolen Fairfax (who has been set the task of studying the history of political economy), to omit the chapter on the fall of the Indian rupee on the ground that it was too sensational. In those who lived through the last quarter of the eighteenth century, unfolding events must have left them giddy. Against a background of unprecedented prosperity (for some), they experienced, in quick succession, the rise of the Irish Volunteers in response to the perceived threat of French invasion, the idea of the Protestant nation, Grattan's Parliament and the intoxication of the American and French revolutions. In the North of Ireland, in particular, these events occurred against a background of widespread and unprecedented literacy and politicisation among the ordinary people. Not only were the United Irishmen the first democrats, they were also thoroughly in the spirit of the Enlightenment in their use of their newspaper, pamphlets, reading societies, ballads and associations as means of propagating their views.

The history being made in America and France bore directly on events in Ireland. Especially in Belfast, an increasingly confident and prosperous Presbyterian middle class could observe these events, empathise with them, and draw lessons for their own situation. The United Irishmen were the first to foster interest in the

Irish language by publishing a miscellany of Irish-language writing, *Bolg an tIolair*. On an international level they can lay claim to having helped to shape the democratic spirit and lack of deference of the burgeoning Australian colony. Several of their banished leaders, Thomas Addis Emmett, William Sampson, James McNeven, John Chambers and David Bailie Warden, made a lasting mark in the young United States to where they had been exiled.

The United Irish movement was the first and last time that Protestants and Catholics in Ireland united themselves in significant numbers in a substantive common political project. Circumstances pitted religious groupings against each other in an unprecedented way. In Wexford it was relatively straightforward: Catholic versus Protestant. In Antrim and Down it was Presbyterian versus Anglican. What is of almost wistful interest for us is that the events of June 1798 in Antrim and Down had almost no sectarian undertones. It should be noted, however, especially in east Antrim, that the failure of the Catholics of Randalstown to rise left a sour taste in the mouths of the Presbyterian rebels around Larne and the Broad Lough. 'Hell roast Randalstown' was a fireside curse for decades to come. More significant, the abject failure of revolt in east Antrim strengthened the sense of disillusionment with the republican ideal.

Northern Catholics played a subordinate role in the events of 1798. Yet within a few generations the vast majority of the descendants of the Presbyterian insurgents were firm unionists while the legacy of republicanism had become claimed by Catholic nationalism which, in the north, had had almost no record of involvement in 1798. It must be one of the most striking examples of the exchange of political clothing in European history. The present-day 'republican' stronghold of west Belfast can lay a tenuous claim to Bartholomew Teeling alone as the only significant Catholic United Irishman who came from the Belfast area. Belfast saw little action in 1798. The dogs didn't bark in Belfast, or in Dublin or Derry either.

Some revisionist historians have criticised the leaders of the

United Irishmen for their dilettante attitudes, for the alleged shallowness of their political ideals, and for having few ideas about changing social structures, at least as expressed in the pages of the *Northern Star* or in the views of the major protagonists such as Wolfe Tone, Samuel Neilson or Henry Joy McCracken. The charge of dilettantism is the one most easily dismissed. The commitment of people such as Tone, McCracken, Neilson, and Jimmy Hope to the cause of revolution after 1795 was total. Tone took his family to and from America and thence to France, a most difficult task in those days, given the prevailing modes of transport. McCracken was a scion of one of the richest and most influential families in Belfast with, to use the contemporary parlance, 'every advantage of person'. He was strikingly handsome and personally attractive in every way. He could have had the easiest of lifestyles (though he appeared to have little time for commercial business). He spent years in the grinding work of clandestine political organisation in the United Irishmen throughout Ulster. Sam Neilson was fond of a drink but unstintingly spent his considerable fortune in the cause. The unswerving and ascetic dedication of Jimmy Hope (known to his contemporaries as 'the Spartan') to the United Irish ideals over decades is well documented.

The fullest articulation of a United Irish view on the prevailing social structures came from Jimmy Hope, the proto-socialist weaver from Templepatrick. Hope's own remarkable political testament, written for Dr Madden more than forty years after 1798, secures his place as a pioneer of working-class democracy in Ireland. He was largely unconcerned about the problems of identity that dominate political discussion today. He was always exercised about social injustice and corruption, about the powerless in society, and about how to restore rights to the people who were the producers in society. But to criticise the United Irishmen for having no social agenda is to miss the point. The United Irishmen were willing to stand up and be counted in opposition to the wholly undemocratic political structures of the time, and that act of defiance was in itself corrosive of the prevailing social structures. Contemporary discourse did not make the twentieth-century differentiation between politics, economics and society. The credentials of the United Irishmen as a progressive force in opposition to the Irish and English oligarchies are secure.

## Lessons of history

Historians have noted that the decade of the 1790s was pivotal in the evolution of modern Ireland. It came at the end of several generations of sustained peace, the longest such interlude in hundreds of years of Irish history. The old Gaelic order had been finally defeated by the Williamite wars, and the long peace of the eighteenth century was born out of exhaustion, prostration and humiliation. By 1801, three years after the rebellion, it became clear that a double defeat had been inflicted, not only on the republican interest, but also on the republicans' immediate adversary, the Protestant Ascendancy entrenched in Dublin Castle. The most immediate and enduring legacy of the failure of rebellion was the 1801 Act of Union, the terms of which have defined Anglo-Irish relations to this day. The political demands of Irish nationalism since that date have centred on the abolition, or modification, of the 1801 act.

Following the Act of Union, Samuel Neilson welcomed the abolition of the corrupt College Green parliament as being a form of political reform. Some Catholics, particularly the hierarchy and the gentry, welcomed the Act of Union as a harbinger of the admission of Catholics to their full political rights. They were to be disappointed, for Catholic Emancipation came only in 1829, and what had been a national question in 1798 had by 1829 become a Catholic one. From 1829 onwards, the delineation of the old reliables of our present-day political landscape was clear: the politics of the sectarian head count, confessional 'majorities' and 'minorities'. All this crowded out the original mass-democratic, non-sectarian ideals of the United Irishmen based on the principles of the rights of men and of nations, as well as of internationalism. The endowment of the Maynooth

College by the British government of William Pitt the Younger in 1795 can be seen, at least in part, as a reward to the Catholic hierarchy for counter-revolutionary support against the radical ideas of the United Irishmen and the threat of French invasion. Throughout the nineteenth century, as the cause of separatism became identified with Irish Catholic nationalism, Maynooth became an intellectual powerhouse for the burgeoning Catholic Church. Daniel O'Connell can be seen as the first Irish populist political leader, and he took the opportunity to shape the forces resiling from the carnage of 1798 and the Act of Union to create a version of Irish Catholic nationalism which, however inadvertently, by implication excluded the Presbyterian and United Irish legacy.

## The puzzle of Presbyterianism

It was not lost on Presbyterians living in Ulster in the first half of the nineteenth century that the first-ever Irish mass movement for political reform under O'Connell focused on the demand for full rights for Catholics and then for repeal of the Union.

For someone from a northern Catholic nationalist background it takes years to get some appreciation of the dynamics, the chameleon-like quality which is inherent in Ulster Presbyterianism. Even today that quality can express itself to the Catholic eye in the annual choice of Moderator. The yearly choice appears to alternate between a Moderator who will participate in ecumenical services with Catholics and one who will not, a kind of 'soft cop/hard cop' routine.

If the ideas of the New Light movement were major formative influences for the United Irishmen generation, they were not the only such influences at work. Even before 1798, Presbyterian reservations and a process of withdrawal from support for Irish republicanism had been strengthened by the rise of Bonapartism in France. By the 1840s, the intellectual climate had radically changed: the pendulum had gone the other way. Henry Cooke had vanquished Henry Montgomery and mainstream Presbyterian thought was being increasingly aligned with the conservative interest.

The strand of Ulster Presbyterianism that is radical has consistently concerned itself with social and economic matters rather than political issues. In the late eighteenth and early nineteenth centuries radicalism in Belfast often expressed itself through schemes for civic improvement such as better paving, sanitation and lighting, a sense of egalitarianism and the drive for educational excellence exemplified in schools such as the Royal Belfast Academical Institution (Inst).

Presbyterianism's espousal of republicanism can be seen to have predated French republicanism and can trace its intellectual origins back to the seventeenth-century English Levellers and even to Oliver Cromwell. But before 1798 it was possible for a radical Presbyterian to be a republican and yet not be a separatist: William Drennan is a case in point. After 1798 the strands of republicanism and separatism were fused together as far as Ulster was concerned.

## The case of O'Connell

The post-1798 transformation of Ulster Presbyterianism was mirrored on the Catholic side. Daniel O'Connell's interaction with the United Irishmen encapsulates a motif for a generational shift in perceptions. O'Connell was twenty-three years old in 1798. He may have been on the fringes of the United Irish movement himself, and he was almost certainly a member of the Yeomanry that were used to crush the rebellion. The lesson he took from the events of the 1790s in both France and Ireland was a lifelong horror of violence and anarchy.

O'Connell, the ruthless advocate of mass mobilisation and 'moral' force, performed many services, and not a few disservices, for Ireland. He himself harked back for political legitimacy to the Irish Volunteer movement. By concentrating on the horrors of the events in 1798, while ignoring the original aims and objectives of the United Irishmen, he helped to crystallise in the popular imagination an image of the United Irishmen as primarily a physical-force movement. The violence of 1798 was remembered: the idealism, the internationalism and the sense of democracy that started its leaders on the road first to reform and then to rebellion were forgotten.

When O'Connell's Repeal movement floundered in futility in the 1840s, his anathematisation of the United Irishmen and the horrors of violence provided a ready-made template in counterpoise for use by, successively, the Young Irelanders, the Fenians and, into the twentieth century, Patrick Pearse and the IRA.

## Sectarianism, paramilitarism and the use of violence

In Ulster immediately prior to 1798 and for decades after, the most visible indication of the entrenchment of popular loyalism and institutionalised sectarianism was the establishment of the Orange Order at Loughgall in 1795. Within two generations the Orange Order, which at its foundation appealed primarily to members of the Church of Ireland squeezed between the Defenderism of the Catholics and the United Irishmen sentiment of the Presbyterians, had become a kind of cleansing room for Ulster Presbyterians where they could slough off any taint of political association with Catholics or ideas of republicanism and separatism. Where the United Irishmen were non-sectarian, the Orange Order was explicitly sectarian in purpose. The effort to create United Irishmen was replaced by a conscious effort to create dis-united Irishmen.

Sectarianism, the idea that political identity is received with one's religious affiliation and that it is not possible to engage in civic life and common purpose with people of another religion on a true and fair basis, has had a dominant influence on political thinking on this island since long before 1798. It has had its most obvious manifestation in the idea that political deals can only be done between major political blocs, and more generally it has had an enervating effect on the universal application and validity of the concepts of civil and religious liberty. This idea of blocs leaves little or no room for diversity of thought, even within each bloc, so further eroding civil and religious liberty.

Some of the blame for the introduction of sectarianism into the political life of the 1790s has been attributed to the United Irishmen themselves; after all, post 1795 they explicitly sought out alliances with the Catholic Defenders in a way that could be seen to compromise their secular cosmopolitanism. Thus, some historians have held, the United Irishmen were responsible, in an inchoate way, for the corruption of their own radicalism and idealism.

Scrutinised more closely, the charge of sectarianism does not hold up. The Irish political elite in *ancien régime* Europe was one of the toughest in Europe and one of the few that withstood the seismic shocks triggered by the fall of the Bastille. Sectarianism was deliberately injected, first by conservative gentry and then by Dublin Castle, into the political scene as a counter-revolutionary weapon. Sectarianism was endorsed and legitimised by a state that was determined to see off the establishment of new political structures that could adequately represent the Irish people in their inherited complexity.

Yet, on another level, the United Irish movement must, *prima facie*, be vulnerable to the charge of partial responsibility (along with the Irish Volunteers) for having ushered in the virus of paramilitarism into the Irish body politic. Our murderous alphabet soup of paramilitary groups can with some justification trace some of their lineage back to the United Irishmen and their latter-day allies, the Defenders. What is more, particularly on the 'republican' side, the lessons of 1798 have been appropriated for repeated acts of bloodshed, irrespective of whether they have moved on 'the cause' one millimetre or not.

John Hume has noted that politically motivated groups in Ireland have consistently resorted to violence because 'it works' and can be justified as the only way to effect political change. Even in the middle of a peace process, and even after acceptance of the Mitchell Principles, in November 1997 Gerry Adams can tell hundreds of his hard-core supporters in the Europa Hotel that they are magnificent: 'you people are literally undefeatable'. This bombast ignores the myriad personal defeats and tragedies inflicted on his constituency over the past generation. Six hundred of his constituents have been killed over twenty-eight years, three-quarters of these by paramilitary groups.

Throughout the nineteenth and twentieth centuries the debate between proponents of differing interpretations of Irish history transmuted itself into a struggle for political legitimacy. That struggle for political legitimacy is lined with the morality or justification of the use of physical force in order to attain political ends. The individual decision as to whether to support or reject the use of violence is a personal decision for every individual. My personal odyssey is briefly dealt with below. The idea of the total commitment of the United Irishmen to physical force was, in Marianne Elliott's words, 'not the only travesty of reality in the developing myth'. As she has noted, few United Irishmen had been doctrinaire republicans, and their record on a programme for social reform was patchy. Indeed, the columns of the United Irishmen's newspaper, the *Northern Star*, record the United Irishmen's opposition to a campaign by striking weavers for better wages.

Viewed through the prism of history as it shifts from generation to generation, little about the United Irishmen is cut and dried. Even the idea of separation from England as expressed by Wolfe Tone ('breaking the connection ... the ever failing source of all our evils') is not as simple as, say, Patrick Pearse would have liked. The United Irishmen were unambiguous in their opposition to the undemocratic English government, but they sought cooperation and partnership with the English people and, by implication, would have embraced partnership with an English government representative of the will of the English people.

Fenianism and twentieth-century physical-force republicanism further drained United Irishmen republicanism of other complexities and subtleties. The United Irishmen expressed no national hatred of England as such, and some of the wilder utterances of Pearse in the name of republicanism would surely have baffled them. The co-option of the United Irishmen by Irish Catholic nationalism from the nineteenth century onwards not only filtered out the self-conscious internationalism of the original movement but transmuted it into a form of chauvinistic nationalism overlaid with the myth of the noble effort. Marking the centenary of Robert Emmet's rebellion, Michael Davitt spoke in 1903 of the 'triumph of failure'. The myth of the glorious defeat was initiated by some of the United Irishmen themselves when they found themselves confronting failure.

The phrase 'glorious defeat' has its own lessons for our generation. Three thousand five hundred people dead has not moved the situation forward one iota. If anything it has undermined for a generation the ideal of the unity of Protestant, Catholic and Dissenter.

The paramilitary inheritors of the United Irishmen tradition of armed rebellion have consistently expressed disdain for the will of democratically elected government whether in Dublin or London. As A.T.Q. Stewart has pointed out, even the hated Stormont parliament remained a parliamentary democracy throughout its fifty years, however grossly imperfect. There is a world of difference between taking up arms against a brutal oligarchy in 1798 and taking up arms in the 1990s against the governments of the British Isles committed by democratic consent to ever closer European union.

The dangers for us are

- acceptance of the myth of 'unfinished business'
- *ex post facto* legitimisation of the act of taking up arms, however courageously, against overwhelming odds
- elevation of the concepts of separatism and national sovereignty into immutable and unyielding principle
- most pernicious of all, the idea articulated by de Valera in 1922 (although, in fairness, later resiled from) that the Irish people have no right to do wrong when they

seek to make political accommodations for their own generation.

Jimmy Hope's characteristically sober remarks on violence have resonance to the present day. Referring to leaders of the rebellion who surrendered and went to England, he says that he does not 'rank them with the common herd of traitors. They were men who unthinkingly staked more than was in them.' For anyone who embarks on any form of politically motivated action, that remark gives pause for thought. For three years after 1798, Hope was on the run, and yet he says:

> Determined never to be taken alive ... I went with a brace of loaded pistols in my breast, but I never discharged them during all that time at any human creature, although I had repeated opportunities. ... I never felt myself justified in shedding blood, except in cases of attack, which it was my good fortune to evade.

And again:

> So complete was the concentration of aristocratic monetary influence, that nothing but its own corruption could destroy it. I remember when power was law, and physical force settled every question. The destruction of the *Northern Star* silenced moral force for a time, and physical force was then resorted to by the people for the preservation of life and liberty. ... Moral force, in its operation, resembles that of Herod's visitation: it ultimately works on the opponents of truth like a consuming worm.

John Gray, present Librarian of the Linen Hall Library and worthy successor to Thomas Russell, has noted: 'One can be cynical about many things in Irish history, but not about the United Irishmen.' The actions of the men of 1798 came from a generous heart. As a recent commentator has acknowledged: 'the rebels died without a blemish on their name. The Presbyterian community gave some of their brightest and best in a cause that was only partly their own.'

There is an aphorism coined by George Santayana that 'those who forget history are condemned to repeat it'. The corollary is that 'those who remember history all too well repeat it on purpose'. What we in our own day can do is to look down the abyss of the past 200 years, in particular the last awful twenty-eight years. Where has the politics of sectarian division got us, or the politics of safety in numbers, or the 'majority takes all' mentality? We should reaffirm Tone's dream, in humility and honesty remember the United Irishmen and consider that even our most cherished perceptions about them might need to be periodically reassessed. What any commemoration can never be is a call to arms.

A PERSONAL DIGRESSION

I was born in a house on Belfast's Falls Road and grew up in Andersonstown in the 1950s and 1960s. There I absorbed the idea that the word 'republican' was inextricably linked with the use of physical force. I was the youngest child of a sceptical socialist father and a 'republican' mother who adored de Valera (after whom I received my Christian name). My maternal grandmother had known Pearse, Connolly and Casement and had been election agent for de Valera in the general election of 1918 when he stood in West Belfast and was beaten by Joe Devlin. My grandmother ran the Falls Road post office (opposite the Falls Road library), an office of profit under the crown. Her support for de Valera in defeat on the day of the result was expressed by the flying of a tricolour from the post office. This so incensed a Devlinite mob celebrating victory that it attacked the building. This is the first and, to date, the only instance in which west Belfast constitutional nationalists intimidated physical-force nationalists.

The experiences of the period 1916–21 left my mother with a lifelong scepticism about the commitment of many of the people on the Falls Road to the original principles of Irish republicanism. She remembered only too well the Union-Jack-waving crowds of workers leaving the Falls Road mills on Armistice Day, 1918. My memory, looking back on the Falls Road of the 1950s and 1960s, is of an atmosphere of repressiveness and a kind of cowed sullenness surrounding any notion of political action. I have a very early memory of my parents' delight at the election of Jack Beattie, a Protestant trade union official, as MP for West Belfast in some kind of Labour interest. In those days, the Westminster parliament was referred to by the BBC and the *Belfast Telegraph* as the 'Imperial Parliament' in order to distinguish it from the home-grown Stormont parliament.

As a child, I sensed the hopelessness and contempt of my elders for anything to do with Stormont, even if there was grudging recognition that some sort of engagement with the system was required in order to have any hope of obtaining a permanent and pensionable job in, say, teaching or the civil service. In order to secure a teaching post, it was necessary to pass a loyalty test imposed by the Department of Education: the requirement to take an oath of allegiance to Queen Elizabeth. This caused many a crisis of conscience, though not in our household where my mother extracted a commitment from us at an early age somehow to secure a profession or vocation that would allow us 'never to take the Oath'. The other rite of passage in securing the imprint of nationality was my mother's determination to ensure that we all learned to speak the Irish language fluently.

The new housing estates of Andersonstown and the Glen Road appeared, even to my childhood eyes, as being totally unplanned for the thousands of young families being decanted into them. Among other deficiencies, they had totally inadequate educational facilities. When I started St Malachy's College, I had to queue for a bus which went down the Falls Road. I alighted at Dover Street for a hazardous ten-minute sprint across the Shankill Road and Peter's Hill.

Two events were notable in shaping my adolescent understanding of Irish history. One was being told (as was almost everyone in the St Malachy's College of the time) that I would never make anything of myself, but not to bother to record (fictionalise is not the proper word) or satirise the casual brutality of many of the teaching staff as 'it has already been done by somebody far more talented than you lot.' The English literature teacher who made that remark was referring to a notorious old boy, the novelist Brian Moore, who was not mentioned much in the respectable Belfast Catholic society of the early sixties: he had committed the grave sin of 'letting our side down'. Seamus Heaney talks about the effects of the 'shock of recognition' when confronted with a piece of literature that has relevance to life as one leads it. My head swam when I read novels such as Moore's *Feast of Lupercal* and *The Emperor of Ice-Cream* about the petty venality of thinly fictionalised characters who were teaching *me*.

A second significant shaping event was my absorption of the ideas I found in James Connolly's *Labour in Ireland*, purchased in McLean's socialist bookshop in Union Street for a few shillings from my Saturday job. Connolly was a master of polemic. He had withering contempt for Daniel O'Connell and admiration for the 'revolutionist' Wolfe Tone who, in Connolly's view, had built his hopes upon the successful prosecution of a class war. Whatever the validity of Connolly's Marxist interpretation, the insight that *Labour in Ireland* left me with was of the internationalism, radicalism and avowedly democratic intent of the United Irishmen. Further reading about the works of Francis Hutcheson, who formulated the basic principle of utilitarianism before Jeremy Bentham, strengthened this insight further.

Another 'shock of recognition' was visited on me by my parents, who told me of the history of Jimmy Hope and pointed out to me neighbours who were descendants of the said Jimmy. One of those descendants was a well-liked Catholic priest, who was my teacher in primary school; it was not explained how the staunchly Presbyterian Hope's descendants had become Catholics, and I still haven't worked this out.

At the same time, there was a sense of bafflement that, while those who rebelled in 1798 were overwhelmingly Presbyterians, the everyday reality of our lives in sixties Belfast brought home to us that Presbyterians were now firmly unionist. Indeed, if anything, Presbyterians were more inclined to be hardline in relation to Catholicism and nationalism than members of the Church of Ireland.

In the Andersonstown of the fifties and sixties, political activity was a circumscribed affair, with Catholics/nationalists taking the role of observers more often than that of participants. I remember a maverick former lord mayor of Belfast who fell out with the Unionist Party establishment and ran as an independent unionist in opposition to the official unionist candidate. The maverick independent calculated that if he could draw in enough votes from nationalists, who had no candidate of their own, he could get himself elected. He targeted a leaflet to houses in Andersonstown listing examples of his supposed partiality to Catholics and nationalists in general. At the bottom, he had cyclostyled the handwritten message 'also attended the funeral of Alderman McEntee'. My parents were greatly amused, my father noting that most unionist politicians were, in principle, happy to attend the funeral of any Catholic as it meant that there was one nationalist vote fewer on the electoral register. Enough Andersonstown voters played along with the game and voted for the maverick alderman; he romped home on election day, to the discomfiture of the unionist establishment.

Except in overwhelmingly nationalist constituencies, Stormont elections were treated with disdain. Apart from a few vaguely Labour Stormont MPs in and around Belfast, the opposition to the unionist majority consisted of a few disparate individualists, some of them effective, some quite awful, who sailed under the flag of convenience of the Nationalist Party. My parents had little time for the Nationalist Party (which resolutely refused to organise, being a confederation of political one-man bands).

The Nationalists had an informal agreement with Sinn Féin that the latter would contest Westminster elections on an abstentionist ticket. During the fifties Sinn Féin had actually won seats at Westminster in Mid-Ulster and Fermanagh-South Tyrone in elections with abnormally high turnouts (sometimes as high as

85 per cent) but its MPs refused to take their seats because of the oath of allegiance and then were disqualified. Sufficient numbers of nationalist voters decided after a few by-elections that the game wasn't worth the candle, and enough stayed at home to ensure that the unionists finally regained the seats.

It was not until 1966 when Gerry Fitt, later to become the first leader of the Social and Democratic Labour Party (SDLP), won West Belfast on a pledge to attend Westminster that fifty years of unquestioned unionist domination was challenged. Up to that point, in my child's mind, being 'republican' equated with being 'Sinn Féin'. Being 'Sinn Féin' meant coming from the countryside and being unknown to most of the population in Belfast. I remember lying in a bed on a summer night listening to a Tyrone voice shouting on the public address system 'Vote Sinn Féin, Treanor's the lad.' Many of my elders hadn't a clue who Treanor was, but plenty of them voted for him, safe in the knowledge that he wouldn't win. Being Sinn Féin also meant being in favour of physical force in order to remove the hated border, the source of all our troubles. It was only as an adult that I realised that the Sinn Féin 'republicans' of the fifties and sixties, even at their best, could be placed in the tradition of defenderism rather than that of the United Irishmen.

In 1956 the IRA started an ineffectual campaign against customs posts and isolated police stations which lasted until 1962. There was little or no IRA activity in Belfast. My sister's boyfriend (later her husband) was one of around three hundred men interned without trial immediately following the commencement of the violence. Ciarán Ó Catháin stayed in jail for three years. While internment was common in the Lower Falls, it was much less so in the more suburban Andersonstown district, and our family became aware of a chill among neighbours. The reaction in my family circle was one of dismay: Ciarán was an Irish-language enthusiast who would have also classed himself as a republican, but a more peace-loving character it was hard to imagine.

Over time, Ciarán's imprisonment made me realise that being 'republican' did not necessarily mean that you were in favour of physical force. I decided very early on that the idea of physical force was not for me. As for Ciarán, on his release he went on to pursue a glittering academic career in civil engineering and business studies. He was instrumental in the voluntary rebuilding of Bombay Street after it had been burned down in the sectarian pogroms of August 1969, and in founding Ballymurphy Enterprises. His untimely death was a tragedy: he was living proof of Jonathan Swift's dictum that a patriot is someone who makes two blades of grass grow where one grew previously. Ar dheis Dé go raibh a anam uasal.

As a teenager I involved myself in the collateral political action generated by the rapid unfreezing of the political structures. As a sixteen-year-old, I leafleted for the Northern Ireland Labour Party, a pro-union sister party of the British Labour Party. Later I joined the National Democratic Party (NDP), a forerunner of the SDLP which explicitly embraced the principle of organisation in all constituencies where there was significant political support. I took part in the first civil rights march on 5 October 1968 in Derry (where I was batoned), and later at the march at Linenhall Street in Belfast. My memory is that few, if any, Sinn Féiners were present, the few hundred demonstrators being mostly students, socialists, communists and NDP.

All this was before the situation exploded in violence in August 1969. Everyone could see the storm clouds gathering but even then, with one brief wavering at the time of the Falls Road curfew in June 1970, I had in my own mind rejected the physical-force ideal. I had reconciled in my own mind that, if being a 'republican' meant being in favour of physical force, then I was not a republican.

# 6

# Pluralism and the Death of Deference

DAVID COOK

Fontevrault l'Abbaye is a small French town, probably more abbey than town, lying south of the Loire near Saumur. The abbey was founded in either 1099 or 1101. The church and most of the buildings are still there and have been gloriously restored. The sunlight striking the sandstone of the interior would remind you of the colour of a Donegal beach.

The great abbey of Notre-Dame de Fontevrault proves an early and most unusual example of gender equality. It housed both monks and nuns. Even more unusual, although the abbey was inspired by the rule of Saint Benedict (or perhaps *because* it was so inspired), the abbess was in complete control. It might be a mistake to read too much into this gender equality or to exaggerate the status of women in Europe in the twentieth century. The post of abbess was for a long time held by, and may even have been restricted to, the daughters (unmarried of course) of the kings of France. It could not be asserted with any confidence that the possible gender equality experienced by the scions of the French ruling class extended very much beyond the gates of the abbey. But it can be said that the objective of achieving equality between citizens is a valid and noble objective. The fact that it may not always, or ultimately, be possible does not make the objective any less valid or noble.

The abbey church contains the tombs of Henry, count of Anjou (Henry II of England), his wife Eleanor of Aquitaine and their eldest son Richard Coeur de Lion (Richard I of England). Henry died in 1189. Your opinion of him is likely to depend on the view you take of a tough and able general, a powerful administrator, and a very energetic man. The date of his death – 'the time against which the memory of man runneth not to the contrary' – probably marks the state of a settled law of real property in the English common law system. Even though not everyone can take advantage of it, the ownership of property is an important freedom, and the vindication of the rights of individuals to own property is an important element in most systems of justice. Henry did much to establish the common law system. He is said to have invented the rule of law which is essential to the achievement of that tranquillity and order without which social, political and legal justice cannot be established. (Devotees of Saint Thomas à Becket may, however, wonder what Henry's real commitment to the rule of law was.) He died a bitter man, having fallen out with his sons. They in turn enlisted the help of different groups of barons. Richard I did nothing to resolve the interbaronial power struggles. Things got worse for his brother, King John, who was ultimately obliged to do a deal with his barons.

Magna Carta was signed in 1215. It was quickly made unworkable by some barons and went through a number of editions leading to a big reissue by John's son, Henry III. Magna Carta has since assumed a prominent and generally well-deserved place in legal and constitutional history. Four centuries after its signing, the Petition of Right (1628) and the Habeas Corpus Act (1679) refer straight back to Article 39 ('No free man shall be arrested or imprisoned or disseised or outlawed or exiled or in any way victimised, neither will we attack him or send anyone to attack him, except by the lawful judgement of his peers or by the law of the land'). It is said that some of the ideas, and even the phrases, used in the United States Constitution are traceable to Magna Carta. We could do with Article 39 in Northern Ireland today.

Ideas about the rights of free men, freedom from victimisation, protection against physical attack, and the rule of law and due process were appearing as early as the thirteenth century. But perhaps the most important thing about Magna Carta was that it was extracted from King John by the barons. The king was to be no more than *primus inter pares* – first among equals. In those days – and in a very few societies and communities still today – the idea of kingship was inextricably bound up with the notion either that the king himself was divine or that the office was ordained by God. Both notions placed the king above the law and beyond the reach of citizens. Although John was obliged to make concessions to his (relatively few) 'equals', the doctrine of the divine right of kings was by no means dead. Charles I was to lose his head on account, *inter alia*, of that doctrine more than four hundred years later. And a correspondent to the London *Times* on 22 November 1997 could still write: 'The monarchy is not a democratic institution, still less the creature of popular opinion, but rather a divinely instituted symbol and mystery.'

The association of kingship with divinity may have done Charles I no good but it would be a mistake to underestimate the power of the idea of the divine right of kings. It is still around today. Internal arguments within ruling elites that have resulted in the deposition, or even decapitation, of kings should not be confused with the arrival of 'the Republic' or even democracy. However 'equal' King John and his barons might have been, they were not living in anything remotely like a democracy. The franchise, if such it could be called, was restricted to about seventy-five royals and noblemen.

Nevertheless, the idea that the rule of law involves citizens who are equal before the law and that justice lies, at least in part, in that equality is an ancient one. But we should not get carried away. Article 54 of Magna Carta states: 'No one shall be arrested or imprisoned upon the appeal of a woman for the death of anyone except her husband.' We have already noted that the position of women in twelfth- and thirteenth-century Europe was not all that great.

The English parliament gave an indication of some incipient republican credentials in 1649 by beheading the king. Prior to the establishment of the Commonwealth in May 1649, it passed acts abolishing both the monarchy and the House of Lords. When parliament was faced, however, with the opportunity to support and develop the ideas of the Levellers who had been debating a range of serious policy issues for some four years, often inside the New Model Army, they would have nothing of it. The generals restored order by force in 1649. Perhaps we should not be surprised. The Levellers argued for: manhood suffrage; redistribution of seats; annual or biannual sessions of parliament; economic reforms for small property holders; decentralisation of government to local communities; complete equality before the law; abolition of trading monopolies; the reopening of enclosed land; security of tenure for copyholders; no conscription or billeting; drastic law reform; abolition of tithes (and so of the state church); and complete freedom of worship.

The poor old Diggers made even less headway. They appeared briefly in 1649 and 1650. Their analysis was that the Civil War had been fought against the king and the great landowners. They proposed that land should be made available to the very poor to cultivate. The Diggers were dispersed in 1650: the landowners put the mob on them. They were even attacked by the Levellers, perhaps because the Diggers called themselves 'True Levellers'. Equality and justice, and the relationship between those ideas and actual policies for their implementation were developing, but ever so slowly.

As for pluralism – the notion that diversity in society is probably inevitable and in any event desirable and that it should be expressly provided for in the systems society adopts for its government (which anyone today might identify as a *sine qua non* for any modern society, whether a republic or otherwise) – it is difficult to see anything remotely approaching it. The fourteenth-century persecution of the Jews in York, the religious upheavals and sectarianism of the sixteenth and seventeenth centuries flowing from Henry VIII's activities, and the Penal Laws of the eighteenth century all suggest that pluralism is a very late invention. We do not need to draw examples from history: pluralism has yet to gain a firm foothold in Northern Ireland.

The monarchy was slow to change. If the regicides of 1649 disposed of Charles I, they were clearly not able to dispose of the monarchy. Indeed, the monarchy bounced back in 1660 and disposed of some of the regicides. But change did come. In the Bill of Rights of 1688, which included a recitation of all the crimes of recent monarchs, the first articles adopted were as follows:

- That the pretended power of suspending laws and the execution of law by regal authority without the consent of parliament is illegal.
- That the pretended power of dispensing with laws or the execution of laws by regal authority as it has been assumed and exercised of late is illegal.
- That levying money for or to the use of the Crown by pretence of prerogative without grant of parliament for longer time or in other manner than the same is or shall be granted as illegal.

The Bill of Rights, confirming the rights of citizens and the supremacy of parliament, represented a vastly important stage in the downgrading of the status of the monarchy. Those rights were accepted by William and Mary as conditions precedent to them being declared King and Queen. That declaration is contained in the last part of the bill. No monarch before them had deferred in this way to parliament. That may be because no monarch before William and Mary had been chosen by parliament. There is obviously no particular reason why the monarch should not be chosen by parliament. After all, if it was good enough for our Billy . . . !

The process of moving the monarchy, like some parties in Ireland, from being slightly constitutional to being constitutional took a long time and was not by any means concluded by the Bill of Rights. It was, after all, the remaining prerogative rights of the crown that George III invoked in America to something less than universal applause. The gradual constitutionalisation of the monarchy in England, however unusual compared with other European monarchies, was connected with the development of a parliamentary democracy. That idea also developed on the Continent and may have had its origins in Geneva.

It is sometimes suggested that John Calvin's influence on political theory was as great as his religious influence. Calvin's importance in the development of Protestantism, even as its founding father, is not necessarily related to what is thought to have been his personal preference for a republic rather than a monarchy. But that preference must surely be connected to his general proposition that the proper responsibility of a state is not only the maintenance of public order but also a positive concern for the general welfare of society. For those who have some difficulty with the proposition either that there is such a thing as a state or that, if there is, the state can itself have a responsibility or a purpose, it may be necessary to ascribe any such responsibility or purpose to groupings of powerful individuals or elites or parties within the state.

Calvin's ideas about church government were important in developing ideas about democracy. The development and, over the centuries, the improvement and refinement of a representative parliamentary democracy are important contributions to the political justice that citizens ought to be able to expect (even if not yet very far advanced in the absence of proportional representation and regional devolution and in the presence of the

House of Lords). The idea of the priesthood of all believers may have come with what some regard as a conservative and limiting way of life but it was a shocking blow to the hierarchical and authoritarian structures of the Church. The idea that individual members of a church might all be equal in its councils did not suit a bishop who was not much given to discussing his ideas with his church members, or a king who liked to govern without too much interference from his subjects. In the days when kings and bishops were both titular and executive heads of government, the emergence of the Presbyterian system of democratic church government was novel, challenging and even revolutionary.

In Ireland that Presbyterian culture remains measurably different from the culture of Catholic Europe (and part of Ireland) and is clearly related to some of the problems we still have to deal with in Northern Ireland. If those cultures either cannot or should not be assimilated in some third culture, and if one cannot or should not be subjugated to the other, a pluralist form of government or way of governing society is the only possible way of proceeding. It is the only possible way of proceeding however complicated pluralism is and however antipathetic it may be to the certainties proclaimed by cultural determinists who assert that there neither can nor should be pluralism in Ireland, and that either Catholic or Protestant values must predominate over the other either because the one set of values is true, or because the other is false, or because we hate 'them', or because if we give an inch we shall be on the slippery slope to a united Ireland, or because the Irish nation cannot be a nation unless it purifies itself against all things British.

The emphasis placed on the freedom of individual conscience in Protestant culture and the importance placed on the value of individuality do not at all mean that individuality is not valued in Catholic culture but do give rise to at least a possibility, perhaps even a certainty, that the structures we must now design for our government in Northern Ireland can be sophisticated enough not simply to permit but also to encourage individual citizens of both or all sorts to thrive within those structures. Sir Isaiah

Berlin's obituarist recently made this point:

> In all his publications and lectures he defended the value which was for him overriding: the value of individuality and human diversity, and of any relaxed social and political conditions which allowed it to flourish. He was suspicious of all general schemes of human improvement that do not take account of the peculiarities of local history and of local social conditions because he believed that they must lead to enforced conformity and therefore to tyranny. He wished eccentricities to be protected when they were both authentic and harmless and unforced national differences to be respected.

On the eve of the French and American revolutions, it was clear that, however imperfect in their realisation, the values of equality, fraternity, liberty and, we may add, justice, were present in the political culture of Europe and America, and were held, at least by some people, to be important. The same cannot be said as surely for the values of individuality and pluralism which may, as I have suggested, be a twentieth-century invention. Nor can it be said that, while egalitarian ideas were around, they were by any means universal. We might however be permitted to remind ourselves that as early as the 1780s the people of Belfast decided that the city was not, like Liverpool for instance, going to be a slave-trading port. Perhaps it was for that reason that the same people were so antipathetic one hundred years later to Gladstone whose family had made its money in slavery in Liverpool. And by the 1780s, one hundred years after the Bill of Rights, and following the development of cabinet-style government, the English monarchy was at least moving in the direction of constitutionality, even though a lot of work remained to be done as Pitt found to his cost when he had the honour to resign in the face of George III's refusal to accept Catholic Emancipation in the immediate aftermath of the Act of Union of 1800.

This is not the place to analyse why the American and French revolutions took place when they did. But it is to the point to remark on some common constitutional themes that emerged from both. The constitution of the United States, declared in 1787, had his preamble:

> We the people of the United States in order to form a more perfect union, establish justice, insure domestic tranquillity, provide for the common defence, promote the general welfare and secure the blessings of liberty to ourselves and our posterity do ordain and establish this constitution for the United States of America.

In France, the first five articles of the Declaration of the Rights of Man and of the Citizen published in 1789 were as follows:

1. Men are born and remain free and equal in respect of rights. Social distinctions shall be based solely on public utility.
2. The purpose of all civil escalation is the preservation of the natural and imprescriptable rights of man. These rights are liberty, property, and the resistance to oppression.
3. The nation is essentially the source of all sovereignty nor shall any body of men or any individual exercise authority which is not expressly derived from it.
4. Liberty consists in the power of doing what ever does not injure another. Accordingly the exercise of the natural rights of every man has not other limits than those which are necessary to secure to every other man the free exercise of the same rights; and these limits are determinable only by the law.
5. The law ought to prohibit only actions hurtful to society. What is not prohibited by law should not be hindered; nor should anyone be compelled to do that which the law does not require.

These are the great republican constitutions. 'We the people' and 'The nation is the essential source of all sovereignty' are still powerful messages. In the case of America the monarchy was deposed, and in the case of France it was dramatically and violently overthrown. But the discomfiture of the monarchy in each case was manifestly not the only thing that was going on. The themes of justice, equality and liberty are spelt out clearly in these constitutions, and the aim of promoting 'the general welfare' and the assertion that 'men are born free and equal in respect of rights' speak of common brotherhood (*'fraternité'*), positive social purposes and a proactivity that go well beyond the essentially negative deposition of the monarchy.

It is not difficult to see where some of the ideas of the Society of United Irishmen came from. Apart from 'Deliverance from the odious influence of England', an analysis of *The Union Doctrine or a Poor Man's Catechism* published after 1798 and thought to contain the 'Catechism of the United Irishmen' discloses the following policies and ideas:

- the right of all Irishmen to own all the land
- the fair division of that land
- the abolition of religious establishments
- the expropriation of church lands
- the introduction of universal adult suffrage
- representative governments
- assemblies or parliaments limited to two years
- equality before the law
- no deprivation of liberty or of property except by law.

The preamble to *The Union Doctrine* refers expressly to 'The Supreme Majesty of the people' and to 'the equality of man'. The connection with events in America and France is direct. The similarity of some of the policies to those of the Levellers 150 years earlier in England is uncanny. The fact that both movements were suppressed by force cannot be a coincidence.

Some thirty years later, Wellington showed how someone who had opposed reform tooth and nail could quite comfortably accommodate it after the great Reform Bill of 1832; later in the nineteenth century, Disraeli, in particular, demonstrated the political art of actually stealing his opponents' policies. So also with monarchs. They either adapt or die. There was a time when the king was the state. Louis XVI said, 'L'Etat c'est moi.' It was no idle boast, but it has long since ceased to be the case with other

European monarchies who avoided the fate of their French counterparts. Later again, the ability not to stagnate explains how most European states avoided the drama of the Russian Revolution. The willingness or simply the ability to promote or at least acquiesce in change disarms all sorts of opposition. This is a lesson that might yet be absorbed by our own political elites in their inter-party talks going on at Stormont Castle.

The definitions of the words 'republic' or 'republican' throw up some interesting distinctions between the mere absence of a monarchy and what else is going on. Dr Johnson in 1755, quoting Addison, gives the following definition:

> *Republican* – One who thinks a commonwealth without monarchy be the government.

Dr Johnson sets alongside this definition one that is attributed to Burke:

> *Republican* – placing the Government in the people; approving this kind of Government.

Dr Johnson returns to Addison with the following:

> *Republic* – Commonwealth; a State in which the power is lodged in more than one.

The *Shorter Oxford English Dictionary* has, *inter alia*:

> *Republic* – A state in which the supreme power rests in the people and their elected representatives or officers, *as opposed to* [my emphasis] one governed by a king or the like ...

All these definitions surely emphasise that a republic does not consist merely in the absence of a monarch but involves the people in government and what we might describe, in short, as a representative parliamentary democracy. Webster offers these among its definitions:

> *Republic* – A government having a chief of state who is not a monarch and who in modern times is usually a president.

> *Republic* – A government in which supreme power resides in a body of citizens entitled to vote and is exercised by elected officers and representatives responsible to them and governing according to law.

The first is clearly the popular understanding of a republic. The second confirms the earlier point that much more is involved and adds, for good measure, that the government shall be 'according to law'. This may remind us of Magna Carta and the Bill of Rights.

The idea that a form of government or a state, in this day and age, is simply either a monarchy or a republic and that one is necessarily or automatically better than another is surely an inadequate description of the sort of society that most citizens wish to achieve. The question of whether the head of state should be hereditary or elected is an interesting one and may even be preceded by the question of whether a head of state is needed at all. I will return to both questions later. In the meantime, let us return to the question of the establishment of justice and the equality of man, which as we have seen are central purposes of the French and American constitutions. Some may take the view that the achievement of perfect justice and perfect equality is not possible, or even that the two are, at least in part, incompatible both with each other and with freedom, but it should be asserted that the achievement of a just society (whether for individuals or groups and whether legal, political, social or economic) has for long been a significantly more important purpose or objective for society to pursue than has been anxiety about the particular nature of the head of state.

Let us dispose fairly quickly of the question of whether a head of state is needed at all. Although the contrary view may be argued, in the sense that there are those who would prefer it otherwise, we may assume that mankind and womankind in any society and community, whether large or small, either like or need or will in any event produce leaders. I am not here talking about the political processes that produce what we know as a prime minister (although there is some anthropological connection between the two) but rather the social processes that require or produce someone in the community to take charge of the ceremonies of that community. Ceremony in society is important, and even if not important it is either desirable or inevitable or both. A head of state is either desirable or necessary or inevitable for the purpose of conducting the ceremonies of the state.

The assertion that the head of state should have ceremonial functions only is of course a far cry from say, Henry II, who was to all intents and purposes 'the state'. Without him there was no government, no army, no judiciary, no administration and no order of any sort. What is more, he was all these things by divine right. The view that the monarch should have ceremonial functions only is obviously a less far cry from the present monarch who is clearly not 'the state' but remains head of the established Church, retains the vestiges of a prerogative power, may – at least on paper – appoint ministers and dissolve parliament, and from whom the crown may pass by heredity to a relation upon the sole condition that that relation is a Protestant.

Should the office of head of state be hereditary? The sad and untimely death of Diana Spencer gave rise to a public debate about the future of the monarchy. Some of this was overblown at the time but its continuing importance should not be underestimated. If there was even a perception (recorded in *The Times* after her brother's oration at her funeral) that not since 1745 had the standard of rebellion been raised so high in Britain, then the debate about the future of the monarchy should, for that reason alone, be taken seriously. I am not myself persuaded that the head of state should not be hereditary although, as I shall describe shortly, I believe the principle can and should be qualified.

There are essentially two sorts of president. The executive sort is perhaps exemplified by the presidents of the United States and France. In these cases I do not believe there is any need to indulge in an argument about whether their system is better or worse than ours. They are merely different and neither theirs nor ours would have lasted as long as it has if they had not adapted over time. The second sort of president, elected but ceremonial only, may be exemplified by Germany and the Republic of Ireland. In the case of the latter, much was made during the 1997 presidential election campaign of the fact that the successful candidate was the nominee of the government parties with clear and robust views about a range of social and constitutional issues, but would on election, in accordance with long-standing practice and the constitution, be required to leave aside those positions and serve and represent everyone in the Republic. This may be very proper and correct, but why necessarily go through a conventionally robust and partisan election campaign? The answer may well be that this is how the Republic of Ireland has chosen and wishes to ordain its affairs. We need enquire no more into it. We do not need to say that one country's system is better or worse than ours – merely that it is different. In the UK, we have a system for producing a head of state that has been remarkably successful for the best part of a millennium, but which has changed dramatically in that time. We should not be afraid of asking whether there are changes that we might now want to make. After all, during the same millennium lip service only has been paid to the hereditary principle. Some monarchs have themselves interfered with heredity by disposing of rivals. And when it has suited either the ruling class or parliament, they have on several occasions switched horses. We can indeed be content that when the present government entertained the Queen and an interesting cross-section of the people to lunch in the Banqueting House in Whitehall in 1997 on the occasion of her fiftieth wedding anniversary, no one felt the need to remind anyone present that Charles I had walked to his execution in 1649 through the room where lunch was served. There is clearly nothing sacrosanct about the hereditary principle. It hardly amounts to anything more than a device invented by most ruling classes in most societies at most times to avoid arguments about who is to succeed to the almost untold wealth and privilege of one of the plum jobs society has to offer. But if, as with the abdication of Edward VIII in 1937, the ruling classes come to the conclusion that change is required, the hereditary principle will, like Charles I, be out of the window, and they will act with speed and ruthlessness.

If the achievement of political, social and economic justice for the members of the society in which we live is or ought to be the core human objective in this life, the method we adopt to choose the head of state, after all for ceremonial purposes only, is comparatively very much less important. The ideal republic does not necessarily require the elimination of all aspects of the hereditary principle in choosing its head of state. But if abolition is not required, reform most certainly is and a good dose of demystification of the monarchy might do us all a lot of good. Reform should cover two different aspects of the monarchy: the job description and the system for passing the job on.

The key to the job description is that the duties of the monarch should be ceremonial only. Providing dignified and ceremonial welcomes for foreign heads of state is a valuable and proper service to provide on behalf of citizens. So also are all the ceremonies and occasions that recognise and honour the many and varied contributions that citizens make to society at large. The monarchy should also very properly continue to be the nonpartisan focus of the loyalty of the armed services. The crown need not, however, retain any prerogative powers, and since the Church of England should in any event be disestablished, the headship of the church need not continue. Parliament should be supreme and should not require a state opening by the monarch. The Queen's Speech is a fiction and should be discontinued. Acts of parliament should be acts *of* parliament and should not require the monarch's signature. But, as already indicated, ceremony is important and national ceremony should be led by the head of state who, in our case, does it very well. The head of state will require a partner to assist but should not require an extended list of 'his sisters and his brothers and his cousins and his aunts'. The present royal family should be reduced in size to the head of state and his or her partner. We sometimes seem to have an oligarchy (self-perpetuating at that) rather than a monarchy, and that was never part of the deal. The grandeur and the assets of the head of state need to be set at appropriate levels. There is no need for a significant number of royal palaces. They should become part of the national heritage.

If the head of state does not need to be elected in a national election and if there is some merit in retaining an hereditary element, how should the succession be organised? First, it goes without saying that it should be desectarianised. Since the Church of England will have been disestablished, no bar would need to be or should be placed on the succession on account of religion. It is proper that any citizen (all references to subjects will be deleted from the law) who holds any sort of office or who exercises any functions or powers over or affecting fellow citizens should be accountable in some way to those citizens. Some accountability should be applied to the monarchy. One way of doing this would be to provide that the succession could be open to any person who is a descendant of, say, George v and who would be between the ages of thirty and fifty when taking the job on. The job could be done for ten or fifteen years, and the successor (from amongst the class of persons mentioned) could be nominated by the government of the day and would be required to obtain the support in a secret ballot of two-thirds of an electoral college consisting of the members of parliament, the members of the second chamber (the successor to the House of Lords, all titles by then having, as in France since the revolution, no status in law), and the members of such devolved regional assemblies in the UK as have come into existence. The disestablishment of the Church of England, the abolition of the legal recognition of titles, the removal of the remnant of the royal prerogative, and the establishment of the real supremacy of the people and elected representatives in parliament as the predominant power in the land will do much to remove the unhealthy deference that is part of the society in which we live. There should be a law against tabloid newspapers publishing stories about whether the wife of the prime minister should be taken to task for wearing trousers when meeting the head of state.

The death of deference is a necessary component of political justice. The civility and respect that citizens who are 'free and equal in respect of rights' properly owe to one another should not be confused with deference. The distinction may not be easy or comfortable to achieve. Such civility and respect is likely to involve some diminution in liberty but that will not be confused with deference in a society where equality and justice are recognised as noble, if difficult, objectives to pursue and where the law sets out to vindicate those objectives. If I am under pressure not to march in semi-military fashion through another man's village, do I show my respect for him by not doing so, or do I defer to him? The actions that flow from a respect for fellow citizens, which in turn may flow from civil civic relationships based on equality and justice, may in some cases be indistinguishable from the actions that flow from showing deference, but the citizen who is being shown respect will know the difference and is much more likely, as a result, to honour the citizen who is doing the respecting. So also with our rulers. The respect and civility that will properly be shown to a head of state who is the first among equals carrying out ceremonial functions will be readily distinguishable from a forelock-tugging deference which is demeaning, unjust and embarrassing.

There is a statutory form of deference which should also be tackled. It is an interesting enquiry, but not immediately relevant here, whether the feudal system, much relied on by Henry II but formally abolished, at least in respect of land tenures, in 1660 in fact involved a form of slavery. All ranks in a highly stratified society (not by any means destratified today) from the king down were obliged by law and custom to render services (later turned into payments in money or kind) to their immediate superiors in the social, political and military chain. This also involved giving allegiance and the swearing of oaths of allegiance and loyalty. It could fairly be said that oaths were taken much more seriously then than now, and since an important part of the feudal system was to do with raising armies for waging wars and crusading against infidels, personal loyalty to the military commander, and a certain discipline were necessary. The notion of allegiance and the oaths relating to it are throwbacks to the feudal system. Happily, they were largely dispensed with in 1868 when Gladstone and parliament made them unlawful for all but a few categories of person. Further reform is desirable, not in relation to oaths (which some, believing in God, are content to make providing that affirmation is possible for those who do not or who prefer not to make oaths) but in relation to allegiance.

The concept of allegiance is not easy to grasp. In that there remain some occasions on which oaths of allegiance are required to be sworn (including by newly elected members of parliament), they still have a legal or quasi-legal existence and status. But for the correspondent to *The Times* for whom the monarchy remains to this day 'a divinely instituted symbol and mystery' I suspect that the notion of acknowledging oneself to be in a state of allegiance is also an emotional and mystical experience. I decline to accept that my contract with the society of which I am a member or the state of which I am a citizen can or should include mystery or mystique or anything that requires a particular emotional response. To be required in any circumstances as a citizen to declare allegiance to a government or a society or a state or a head of state (who is a fellow citizen and who can be no more than *primus inter pares*) is improper and demeaning. I am born into this society the equal of all other persons in it including the head of state, who is not above the law. I am either content or have no alternative but to live in that state in accordance with the customs of civil and civic society and the law. I should not be required to declare any loyalty or allegiance either to another citizen or to the state. As I come of age it will be apparent that my personal attributes, good, bad or indifferent, are likely to differ from those of all other citizens. Such unevenness in ability does not render me or them any less or more equal in terms of rights and duties.

The state of which I am a citizen, or the power elites that are thrown up by the society that forms that state, will over the course of my lifetime pursue a thousand different political policies. I will agree with some and not with others. I may even play a part in promoting some of those policies, but my right to dissent and the freedom to do so without being victimised (see Magna Carta) is one of the most precious liberties I possess. If the state of which I am a citizen chooses to go to war (the extreme case that may require me to subjugate my right to dissent for the common good), my decision to support that policy, or not as the case may be, will be based on whether I think it is right, and not on whether the head of state requires me to, or expects my allegiance. My citizenship is mine by heredity. It is not mine by some act I have to perform such as jumping through a hoop. The equal citizenship I share with other citizens, including the monarch, is my birthright. It cannot and does not depend on some act of allegiance. Citizenship should not be subjected to such tests, and still less should citizens be required to demonstrate loyalty or allegiance to parliamentary institutions. My respect for the head of state is likely to be increased rather than diminished if I am not obliged to subscribe to the feudal mystery of declaring allegiance. This is especially so in a society where those who crow loudest about loyalty and allegiance reserve the right to withdraw them from a monarch who does not remain Protestant. All oaths of allegiance should be abolished.

If respect and deference may merge in a society of equals, the line between believing and not believing in God is often drawn more clearly, even if large numbers of agnostics stand together on that line. The question of whether God exists is likely to continue to exercise the minds of mankind and womankind for some time to come. We may even venture the opinion that it will continue to occupy their minds until, some millions of years ahead, the sun gets too hot or too cold for us and we come to an end. To assert that the end of human life will mean that the question of whether God exists will cease to be an issue would be tendentious, and its validity may in any event depend on whether other people in the solar system have formed a view that God may exist.

A question that is less tendentious, but which will nevertheless raise the temperature, is whether the constitutions of men and women living in society should contain any reference to God? What is or should be the connection, if any, between the constitution of any society and God? The American and French constitutions framed in the last quarter of the eighteenth century, at the height of the Age of Enlightenment, made decisive breaks with the old myths that heads of state ruled by divine right and that citizens may only create constitutions by the grace of God. The preamble to the articles of the Declaration of the Rights of Man and the Citizen that were quoted above refers to the National Assembly of France declaring those rights 'in the presence of the Supreme Being'. This is clearly borrowed from the Freemasonry of the Enlightenment and in historical context could be taken as a deliberate non-reference to God. We should not therefore be surprised that neither the US nor the French constitution makes any reference to God. This is not of course to say that God does not exist or that religion may not be practised. The practice of religion is carefully protected in both cases. These constitutions do, however, establish precedents of enormous importance for the general proposition that it may be proper to leave to Caesar the things that are Caesar's and to leave to God the things that are God's.

If the Church of England were to be disestablished and the head of state were not to be head of that church, I am not aware of any provision or aspect of the British constitution, slippery as that may be to get hold of, that implies or recognises the existence of God or requires the deference of citizens *in their capacity as citizens* to a deity. One of the freedoms I enjoy is that the state of which I am a citizen does not require my deference to God. The Society of United Irishmen does not appear to have required any such deference either. The preamble to the *Union Doctrine* makes no reference to any sort of God and even asserts that 'religious distinctions are only protected by tyrants'. Later, in the 'Catechism', there is only one reference to each of the Creator, the Almighty, and God, and on each occasion it is in the context of suggesting that the entity concerned could only be intended to favour fairness and equality between citizens. Wolfe Tone's

'Declarations and Resolutions of the Society of United Irishmen of Belfast' of October 1791, published not long after the National Assembly of France's Declaration of the Rights of Man and of the Citizen, makes no reference either to a God or to a supreme being. The third of these resolutions — 'That no reform is practicable, efficacious or just which shall not include Irishmen of every religious persuasion' — may be not only the first clear statement of a pluralist vision for Ireland but also a timely reminder of what was lost in the subsequent two hundred years and remains to be found today.

Not all modern constitutions are the same. The first sentences of the preamble to the 1960 Canadian Bill of Rights is in the following terms: 'The Parliament of Canada affirming that the Canadian Nation is founded upon principles that acknowledge the supremacy of God, the dignity and worth of the human person and the position of the family in a society of free men and free institutions ...' The preamble to the Basic Law of the German Federal Republic refers to 'The German People ... conscious of its responsibility before God and men...' This seems to be a measurably less than ringing declaration of the supremacy of God. It may even imply some equality between God and man, or at least that deference of the one for the other is not required.

The constitution of the Irish Republic does not actually use the work 'supremacy' but the several references to God in the Irish constitution amount to something similar, and the deity's supremacy is emphasised by repetition. The references are contained in the preamble and in a number of articles:

PREAMBLE

In the Name of the Most Holy Trinity, from Whom is all authority and to Whom, as our final end, all actions both of men and States must be referred; We, the people of Éire, Humbly acknowledging all our obligations to our Divine Lord, Jesus Christ, Who sustained our fathers through centuries of trial, Gratefully remembering their heroic and unremitting struggle to regain the rightful independence of our Nation, And seeking to promote the common good with due observance of Prudence, Justice and Charity, so that the dignity and freedom of the individual may be assured, true social order attained, the unity of our country restored, and concord established with other nations, Do hereby adopt, enact, and give to ourselves this Constitution.

ARTICLE 6(1)
All powers of government, legislative, executive and judicial, derive, under God, from the people, whose right it is to designate the rulers of the State and, in final appeal, to decide all questions of national policy, according to the requirements of the common good.

ARTICLE 44(1)
The State acknowledges that the homage of public worship is due to Almighty God. It shall hold His Name in reverence, and shall respect and honour religion.

The final words of the constitution (interestingly not translated into English in the English-language version) are: 'Doduum Gloire De agus Onora na hEireann' (To the Glory of God and the honour of Ireland).

The sixty years that have elapsed since the constitution was adopted in 1937 have seen a decisive (although not theoretically irreversible) shift in the constitutional ethos of the Republic of Ireland, especially in the course of the last decade. Change in the law and constitution in relation to divorce and abortion, and the political challenge to the authority of the bishops have been dramatic. But in spite of those changes it may be thought tendentious, and even barely possible, to raise the question of whether the Irish constitution of 1937 in fact created what amounted to a collegiate monarchy where the college was the hierarchy of the Church. Moreover, the certainty following the May 1998 referendum that articles 2 and 3 of the constitution will be altered, is not likely to give rise to any discussion about whether the Irish people will continue to wish to defer to God either at all or in such ringing terms.

The 1937 constitution is of course much longer than the 1916

Proclamation of the Irish Republic, which contains only five short paragraphs. The first and last paragraphs open respectively with the words 'In the name of God and of the dead generations...' and 'We place the cause of the Irish Republic under the protection of the Most High God...' At the end of the twentieth century we are entitled to be disappointed, if not in fact infuriated, that some aspects of the Enlightenment, which contributed so distinctly to the 'Declaration and Resolutions of the Society of United Irishmen of Belfast' in 1791 and which appear to have been consistently ignored by some Irish republicans in the intervening two centuries, show only hesitant and flickering signs of returning now.

Who can say what is a true republic? Is it necessarily a state in which heredity should play no part in the selection of a head of state? Is it necessarily a state in whose constitution no reference to God should appear? Surely there are more important matters requiring our attention. Liberty, equality and fraternity (and we might add justice) are noble objectives even if not perfectly realisable and even if, in some cases, they may be mutually exclusive. The ideal republic must surely be the product of a society in which the declared purpose and settled long-term intention of a sufficient majority of citizens are the achievement of justice and equality; and the creation of social and political structures that allow for and encourage diversity and respect, and bring an end to deference: in short a pluralist state. In the new republic, citizens would show hitherto-unknown levels of tolerance to other citizens in their diversity. That tolerance might very well extend to respect for the eccentricity of those citizens who remained more comfortable with a hereditary element in the process for selecting the head of state, or who preferred to see a reference to God in the constitution.

The abbey at Fontevrault remained a religious house until 1789. During the French Revolution it became a prison and so it remained until it was closed in 1963. It has since become, gloriously, a cultural centre serving the social and civic needs of the northwest of France. So, the abbey is still there but the use to which it has been put has changed. There is no reason why Northern Ireland must or should cease to exist. There is every reason why what goes on in it and its relationship with the Republic of Ireland should change, and we may even suggest that such changes are a precondition to its continued existence. Change is the human condition. It is both possible and inevitable. The achievement of a just society will require change and a lot of energy. Why waste energy worrying about relatively unimportant matters such as a hereditary element in the method of selecting a head of state or whether all references to God should be deleted from the constitution? In the pluralist heaven, many angels can dance on the point of a republican needle.

# 7

# Republicanism Revisited

AVILA KILMURRAY
AND MONICA McWILLIAMS

In a recent study of republican philosophy, the philosopher Philip Pettit argues that the republican concept of freedom should be seen as the 'non-domination' of individuals and collectives. Thus

> Freedom as non-domination requires that a person not be exposed to the possibility of interference on an arbitrary basis.... The idea is dynamic. The notion of what makes an exercise of power arbitrary is systematically developmental.... To endorse republican freedom is not to accept a ready made ideal that can be applied in a mechanical way.... It is to embrace an open-ended ideal.[1]

It is perhaps the tragedy of Irish republicanism that it became a product fast-frozen by nationalism, to be transferred from one generation to the next, with the appropriate brand names attached.

This apparent victory of the mechanical has led at least one political analyst to query whether 'Irish republicanism was to become a synonym for Irish nationalism. Or to put it another way, the idea of a Republic became less an end in itself, than a means towards a nationalist end.'[2] It would seem that this assertion begs three questions. How valid is the concept of republicanism as an end in itself? How feasible is it to disentangle republicanism from nationalism in the context of Ireland? And what value has a revisited dynamic concept of republicanism and, more specifically, civic republicanism? This contribution seeks to initiate a discussion around these questions, and to consider them against the complex backdrop of our historical legacy and the challenges that currently demand attention.

THE HISTORICAL LEGACY

Republicanism is a word to conjure with in Ireland – whether North or South. Emotions and interpretations around the concept, and more important in relation to its implications, are as divided as the island itself. Whether it is defined by the most recent wall slogans in nationalist west Belfast, or is rubbished by a historical revisionism that is tortured by the Yeatsian quandary 'Did that play of mine send out certain men the English shot?', the arguments around republicanism are still fought with vigour.[3]

In 1974, a Repsol pamphlet (a reprint of a 1966 edition) was circulated by the Republican Education Department of the then Republican Clubs (later to become the Workers' Party). It held that 'The association of national freedom with a republican form of government originated in the 1798 period. ... Wolfe Tone and the United Irishmen were the first to raise the demand for an independent Irish Republic.'[4] Enter, stage left, the influence of both the American and, more radical, French revolutions which was to be deployed in an Irish setting against the British connection. Indeed in the specific circumstances of Ireland one of the applications of eighteenth-century republican ideology was to be a translation of the individual rejection of arbitrary power to an assumed collective rejection of the exercise of such power by another state – also a feature of the American Revolution. The contemporary use of the terminology 'slavery' and 'oppression' underlined this translation. While separation from Britain was already an issue for the United Irishmen,[5] the commencement of hostilities between Britain and France in 1793, and the introduction of draconian anti-insurgency measures, resulted in an increased emphasis being placed on this strategic aspect. By 1795, Tone, Thomas Russell, Samuel Neilson, the Simms brothers, Henry McCracken 'and one or two more' climbed to MacArt's Fort at the summit of Belfast's Cave Hill, and took a solemn obligation 'Never to desist in our efforts until we have subverted the authority of England over our country and asserted her independence.'[6]

At his trial in 1798, Wolfe Tone was to reiterate his belief in the separatist cause, but to link it with the concept of citizenship which lies at the core of civic republicanism: 'The connexion of England, I have ever considered the bane of Ireland and have done everything in my power to break it, and to raise three million of my countrymen to the rank of citizens.'[7] It was this sentiment that was to be remembered as Tone's epitaph, alongside his call for the unity of Catholics, Protestants and Dissenters in this cause.[8]

What developed over the following two centuries may be described in general terms as the growing hegemony of Irish nationalism. Writing a history of the Irish Republican Army in 1972, J. Bowyer Bell concluded:

> For a few, generation after generation, what Pearse and Connolly began in the name of Tone on April 24th, 1916, is an unfinished legacy – but a clearly defined responsibility. As long as the British border cuts across the Republic of 1916, as long as Ireland and its people are neither free of exploitation

nor Gaelic in tongue and heart, then men will turn to the task as defined by Tone no matter how bleak the prospects: to do less would be to betray the past and deny the future.[9]

The Tone who was so little enamoured with the Belfast Harp Festival of 1792 that he wrote in his diary (13 July), 'The harpers again, Strum, strum and be hanged', might well not recognise cultural aspects of the new republicanism, or even its definition, given the heightened sense of national identity in the new-strung republican quest. What has been described as the 'simple and apostolic tradition of nationalism'[10] has in effect taken root, nurtured by cultural demands, and inspired by concepts of popular sovereignty and national self-determination.

If Ireland was not different from many other European countries in developing a sense of nationalism throughout the nineteenth and early twentieth centuries, the intellectual legacies left by the process have tended to subsume the potentially more radical aspects of late eighteenth-century republicanism. Certainly if the rhetorical benchmark of Irish nationalist hegemony is taken as the 1937 Bunreacht na hÉireann (Constitution of the Republic of Ireland), it is apparent that by the thirties the radical influence of civic republicanism had been all but dispersed by the vision of an Ireland not free only, but Gaelic and piously Catholic as well.

In essence the nationalist hegemony also came to encompass prevailing views about republicanism – even if some elements of the 'republican family' continued to espouse a degree of social and civic radicalism. What was presented to those who remained outside the hegemonic bloc was, in effect, a continuum that ran from a Catholic, Gaelic, ethnic identity at the one extreme to revolutionary radicalism at the other, but held together by the binding force of national separatism. Concepts such as Irish self-determination, the territorial integrity of the island (inherited from British administrative policy), and separation from the (imperialist/neocolonial) influence of Britain, placed the emphasis on the integral nation-state, rather than on republicanism *per se* –

although it was taken for granted that the latter was a code word for, and encompassed, the former.

THE OTHER HISTORY

The apparent seamlessness of the republican tradition has effectively written out of the historical script those in Ireland who could not identify with it. They were characterised as 'vested interests', 'victims of false consciousness', or simply 'reactionary elements': there was neither a confidence in Tone's aspiration to unite Catholics, Protestants and Dissenters, nor much investment made in realising such a strategy. J. Bowyer Bell also probed the political perspective of the Ulster, British, Protestant tradition, identifying that for many

> An united Ireland would be a nationalist Ireland, and as such an Ireland that would be dominated not only by a Gaelic ethos, but by a Catholic one. Only the republicans imagined themselves non-sectarian. They had been misinformed by their own indulgences and hidden agenda; they were Catholic and so acted, defended 'their people', allied themselves with other Catholics in a pan-nationalist front.[11]

In addition to these sentiments, many in the British Ulster tradition felt a deep frustration at the failure by Irish nationalism to either attempt to understand, or take seriously, the position of that tradition as defined in its own terms.

A sense of insecurity and fear was also evident amongst a population who were a minority and a majority people simultaneously – a majority within Northern Ireland (which itself was dependent on an increasingly unreliable British guarantee), but a minority on the island of Ireland.[12] Thus the Northern Ireland state was conscious of its beleaguered position on the island of Ireland, while being fearful of the implications of having a sizeable minority of perceivably disloyal Catholic nationalists within its borders. The latter, in turn, both resented and feared the implications of being treated as distrusted, second-class citizens on 'their own' island. The dividing lines were marked primarily by national identity, ably reinforced by religious persuasion. Civil and religious liberties in practice became relegated to slogans on banners, as they were increasingly undermined by an ongoing sense of political crisis, and became caught up in the contradiction of 'theirs' or 'ours'.

In relation to the Balkans, the writer Michael Ignatieff recently suggested that 'Cosmopolitanism is the privilege of those who can take a secure nation-state for granted.'[13] This might also be held to be true for liberalism. For different reasons the defensiveness of the societies on both sides of the border hindered any effective examination of the concepts intrinsic to radical republicanism. The emphasis for many years in the South was to prove that the state could work within the framework of a relatively conservative nationalism (although entry to the European Union was to open up that society to a wider range of possibilities), while the impetus within Northern Ireland was to ensure that the state survived *per se*. Issues such as civil liberties and social justice, not to mention equity or secularism, came to be seen as optional extras, or even as threats, in circumstances of conflicting and unresolved national dilemmas. These dilemmas were characterised by a dual majoritarian interpretation of self-determination, the one rooted in historic Irish nationalism (as expressed by the Proclamation of 1916, the general election of 1918, and Bunreacht na hÉireann), and the other based on the political pragmatism of a state some seventy plus years in existence, underpinned by the guarantee embodied in the Government of Ireland Act, and the express will of the majority of the citizens within Northern Ireland to remain British.

In reality, political fixation on the dilemmas and contradictions posed by both a divided island and a divided society within Northern Ireland left little energy or space for exploration of the potential of either civic unionism or civic republicanism, however defined. Equally discouraging were the developments of the 1980s, when an increasingly confident Republic of Ireland took refuge in a growing partitionism as the violence of the conflict within the North became both an embarrassment and, at times, a threat. Both the lack-of-interest message conveyed by this position, and a political revisionism that sought easy scapegoats did little to encourage constructive debate within either nationalism or unionism.

THE CHALLENGES OF CIVIC REPUBLICANISM

The classical tradition of civic republicanism saw 'the deliberations and commitments of the whole body politic as integral to the realisation of a free society; that is, a political theory that considered citizen self-rule as the necessary condition of political liberty'.[14] In this viewpoint there is both an acceptance of the intrinsic value of politics to realise that end, and a rejection of arbitrary authority that can confound the project. Tom Paine identified the feudal institution of monarchy as being the epitome of such arbitrariness, and argued that 'Republican government is no other than government established and conducted for the interest of the public as well individually as collectively'.[15] As Pettit warns, the power of the concept of republicanism also includes its dynamic nature, and by the late eighteenth century democratic self-rule and representative government had come to be viewed as the most effective means of furthering liberty.

The struggle to extend the inclusive nature of citizenship was of course to continue throughout the nineteenth and early twentieth centuries (with only a proportion of women being brought into the electorate by the Representation of the People Act which allowed them to vote in the 1918 general election). Within Ireland, however, Wolfe Tone had set the project as being inextricably linked to breaking the connection with Britain. In this way, his philosophy went considerably further than the most recent wall slogan in nationalist Belfast – 'Brits Out – 1798–1998!' For Tone, set in his historical era, the realisation of civic republicanism was, as in America, dependent on breaking the link with Britain, and for the majority of the United Irishmen it was the quest for extended citizenship that took precedence.[16]

Although the demands for an active, inclusive citizenship and national self-determination can clearly be complementary, equally the two are not necessarily associated. In Ireland, the impact of an increasing emphasis on ethno-cultural nationalism, mobilised around a strong sense of national identity that was projected as natural, introduced an exclusive element into the political debate. In essence the onus was placed on those not of 'native stock' (loosely defined as Catholic, Irish) to opt into the nation-in-formation. In practice, as in the case of many other aspiring nation-states, some of the most eloquent advocates of national identity were those who made this deliberate choice. What was in danger of being lost in the process was the recognition that the liberty to develop a political project that would extend effective republicanism meant more than freedom from Britain to be more genuinely Irish.

It is true that over the decades a more radical view of liberty, self-determination and indeed the republican project did continue to exist among a number of self-professed republicans. A case in point is the members of the Republican Congress, who accepted the need to use Irish independence as an essential framework to create an inclusive political arena, to enable engagement in a broader dialogue with the purpose of creating conditions for a more equitable and just society. This is a perspective, however, that has often been forced to the margins of nationalism. It is also a perspective that itself suffers from a certain fixed approach which suggests that the task at hand is 'the reconquest of Ireland', and that once that is achieved, inclusive systems of a progressive nature can be established. In more simple nationalist terms this approach has been summed up in the suggestion that the political project is to 'build the house first, and then we can finish it'.

The core challenge remains of developing a civic republicanism that can include people from all traditions in Ireland in designing the political project. This challenge cannot be answered effectively by the simplistic slogan 'Brits Out' – particularly in circumstances where the nature of the British political system, and indeed of British involvement in Ireland, is quite different from what it was in the eighteenth, nineteenth, or even early twentieth centuries. We need to work for a collective understanding of the current situation before we can change it.

## THE POTENTIAL OF CIVIC REPUBLICANISM

The relevance of civic republicanism in the late eighteenth century was that it answered real needs in the historical context of the time, while offering a freshness of ideas and a vision for the future. While Wordsworth was celebrating the joy of being alive at such a time, politically active Corresponding Societies in Ireland, Scotland and England were adapting republicanism and Jacobinism to local circumstances. Two hundred years later the need for such a powerful combination of vision, strategy and tactics is still required. In order to be effectively inclusive the impetus for this approach must shift back from nationalism to republicanism, and be prepared to accept the benefits of a heterogeneous society, in place of the homogenising myths of national identity. There is also the crucial strategic challenge of how democratic republicanism can deliver on equality while accommodating, and indeed welcoming, difference.[17]

It is now timely to develop work around a new vision for civic republicanism in Ireland – North and South – as the old certainties are being fractured and the diminution of political violence creates the potential for a healing process to commence. We recognise that both these developments will take time, but they may well be facilitated by an inclusive dialogue about the essential elements of any new political order. At a tactical level, however, the process for such a dialogue is important, as active citizenship in this context can often be inclusive in principle, but exclusive in practice. Experience has shown that nationalists all too often have a clear edge in describing their aspirations and long-term political perspectives. Processes must be developed to ensure a parity of participation in the political discourse.

The insights of the women's movement are an important resource in designing strategies and tactics that seek to ensure the reflection of different voices, and in challenging the practical applicability of universalist concepts and abstract visions. For all too long women's experience has been one of being written out of history, or being seen as a token presence. At the flowering of civic republicanism in France, Olympe de Gouges went to the guillotine in 1793 for a tactical miscalculation in promoting her Declaration of the Rights of Woman, written two years previously.[18] Concerns have also been expressed at the manner in which civic republicanism can seem 'To smuggle real live men into the seemingly abstract and innocent universals that nourish political thought. The "individual" or the "citizen" are obvious candidates here'.[19] In short, women have learned the hard way that inclusion cannot be taken for granted, and that lack of accessible transport or childcare can be as effective an exclusionary device as philosophical equivocation or evasion.

At a strategic level it must be accepted that any effective inclusive engagement in a project to develop civic republicanism in practice will only be achieved when there is a basic sense of security established for minorities within the societies that coexist on the island. This sense of security has to be underpinned by effective policies of equality, equity and protection of human rights, while also allowing space and respect for differing senses of identity, allegiance and citizenship. Expressed in the political terms of the wall slogans there needs to be a general acceptance that the current situation dictates that the loyalist calculation of '6 into 26 won't go!' makes more political and mathematical sense than the new Republican Sinn Féin formulation of '6 + 26 = 1!' However, while mathematics is a rigid science, it must also be accepted that politics is dynamic.

If nationalists can no longer rely on demands for an arbitrary imposition of all-island majoritarianism, it must also be accepted that limitations on the exercise of arbitrary power cut both ways. There is an onus on the proponents of a new, porous Northern Ireland to implement a system that will facilitate the development of a shared democracy rooted in the concepts of active citizenship, however that citizenship may be defined by those involved. Active citizenship places an emphasis on people, and encourages political activity and responsibility on a broad participative basis or – phrased in Rousseau's terms – gives a 'share in the operation of one's own life'[20] and the conditions within which that life is acted out. In practical terms the translation of the theory of active citizenship into reality requires not only a responsive system of representative democracy, but also the supplementary processes and structures that can effectively offer a channel and format to the exercise of such citizenship.

The current political movement across the island of Ireland, and within British–Irish relationships, provides a timely context for the development of more imaginative and inclusive approaches. It is crucial, however, that the professional class of politicians develop the self-confidence not to fear the implications or impact of a more genuinely participative politics. Recent proposals for the Northern, and the North–South, Civic Forums are but an experimental step in this direction. In essence such proposals are based on a redefinition of what might be considered as 'political' in the classical sense; they attempt to renegotiate a balance between representative democracy and the politics of difference.

The dynamic concept of civic republicanism can accommodate a politics of difference within the important parameters of non-domination and the attempt to develop a dialogue around the aspiration of a common good. As the feminist theorist Iris Young has argued, 'We must develop participatory theory not on the assumption of an undifferentiated humanity, but rather on the assumption that there are group differences and that some groups are actually or potentially oppressed or disadvantaged.'[21] The challenge is to create a complementarity of approach that facilitates the representation of these differences alongside the more traditional representative democracy. Citizenship must encompass both individual equity and more specific group concerns that are often in danger of being relegated to the outer reaches of political denial.

While there are clear dangers in institutionalising group representation, there is a need to examine how those groups that have been most excluded from the political process can both be facilitated to formulate an input into policy and be actively enabled to participate in a politics of inclusion. Strategies to address this issue would effectively build a real sense of citizenship that would go far beyond any ascribed sense of national hegemony. Active citizenship and participation would be based on the articulation of real needs and concerns, rather than on a fear of not sharing a national identity.

Returning to Pettit's portrayal of civic republicanism as 'an open-ended ideal', it does seem to us to be a valuable concept which allows for a new dialogue, and opportunity for engagement, around what people might envisage and aspire to in the future. Civic republicanism seeks allegiance on the basis further outlined by Pettit:

> We can surely identify with the republican polity for the fact that it gives each of us, and each of us to the extent that it gives all, the measure of non-domination that goes with being a fully incorporated member; a fully authorised and a fully recognised citizen. If we cherish our citizenship and our freedom, we have to cherish at the same time the social body in the membership of which that status consists.[22]

In other words there is the responsibility of a quid pro quo which hopefully allows us to go beyond the 'them' and the 'us' both within Northern Ireland, and between North and South. If civic republicanism can help us achieve this, the concept is a valuable one.

It is clear, however, that if this process is to be inclusive it must go beyond the fast-frozen nationalist objectification of Ireland and the Irish. While the past deserves to be judged on its own terms, the Cathleen ni Houlihan of the 1990s is more likely to be on a plane to Brussels than to be patiently, if mournfully, awaiting rescue by the heroic invariably male figure of historical myth. The deliberate bolstering of a sense of ethnicity by both majority and minority communities within Northern Ireland since the mid-1980s has been less than helpful when it has been projected in an exclusive manner. It is, nevertheless, just possible that there is now a window of opportunity to replace the complex mix of insecurity and triumphalism with an attempt at an honest dialogue about the implications of post-nationalist republicanism. This may allow us the room to seek a resolution of the unresolved national question within a different, and more positive, dimension.

This then is the value of a revisited dynamic concept of civic republicanism. It can offer the basis for the development of a shared vision of a new politics on a shared, if still disputed, island – with the additional guarantee for the unionist population of an ongoing relationship between Britain and the island of Ireland. There is the possibility that the elements of dispute can themselves be eventually transcended by a political system that creates the space for a sense of belonging that stretches beyond exclusive identities. This is not to discount the very real fears, uncertainties and difficulties that must still be taken into account, but it also recognises that any new politics must address values and tasks that cannot be constrained by current boundaries or borders. In this way a dynamic sense of civic republicanism can help us meet the challenge in the new millennium of updating Wolfe Tone's task of uniting Catholic, Protestant and Dissenter 'in the common name of Irishmen', by seeking to unite the population of the communities and identities that comprise this island in the common good of developing a society that can address effectively the requirements of equity, inclusion and human rights.

## NOTES

1. P. Pettit, *Republicanism: A Theory of Freedom and Government* (Oxford: Clarendon Press, 1977), p. 147.
2. R. Kearney, *Postnationalist Ireland* (London: Routledge, 1977), p. 35.
3. W.B. Yeats, 'A Terrible Beauty is Born' in *The Collected Poems of W.B. Yeats* (London: Macmillan, 1961).
4. *Republicanism Part 1, 1790–1922* (Dublin: Repsol Pamphlet No. 8, 1974).
5. The Life of Theobald Wolfe Tone edited by his son (Washington, 1826), cited in M. McNeill, *The Life and Times of Mary Ann McCracken 1770–1866* (Belfast: Blackstaff Press, 1988).
6. O. Knox, *Rebels and Informers: Stirrings of Irish Independence* (London: John Nurray, 1997), p. 158.
7. Knox, p. 257
8. T.W. Tone, *Memoirs* (1) cited in Knox. Tone nevertheless had a degree of concern over the influence of Catholic priests, whom he described as 'low bred rustics of vulgar sentiment'.
9. J. Bowyer Bell, *The Secret Army*, (London: Sphere, 1972), pp. 435–6.
10. 'The Making of Modern Irish History', in D.G. Boyce and A. O'Day, eds., *The Making of Modern Irish Hisory: Revisionism and the Revisionist Controversy* (London: Routledge, 1996).
11. J. Bowyer Bell, *Back to the Future: The Protestants and a United Ireland* (Swords: Poolbeg, 1996), pp. 12–13.
12. Minority Rights Group, cited in T. Hylland Eriksen, *Ethnicity and Nationalism* (London: Pluto Press, 1993), p. 121.
13. M. Ignatieff, cited in M. Canovan, *Nationhood and Political Theory* (Aldershot: Edward Elgar, 1996).
14. N. Porter, *Rethinking Unionism* (Belfast: Blackstaff Press, 1996), p. 107.
15. T. Paine, 'The Rights of Man', cited in Pettit, p. 202.
16. See the letter of William Drennan cited in Knox, p. 85: 'Our present pursuits ought to terminate in an equal and impartial representation of the people, and let posterity go on to republicanism if they choose.'
17. For further discussion of this important question see A. Phillips, *Democracy and Difference* (Cambridge: Polity Press, 1993), pp. 90–103.
18. Olympe de Gouges was executed as a royalist sympathiser for appealing to Queen Marie Antoinette to speak out in the name of all women – a serious mistake under the circumstances.
19. Phillips, p. 77.
20. Jean Jacques Rousseau, cited in P. Barry Clarke, *Deep Citizen* (London: Pluto Press, 1996), p. 23.
21. Young, cited in Phillips, pp. 95–6.
22. Pettit, p. 260.

# Notes on the Contributors

DAVID COOK is former lord mayor of Belfast (1978–9) and was deputy leader of the Alliance Party, 1980–4. He was also chairperson of the Northern Ireland Police Authority from 1994 to 1996.

EAMON HANNA is former general secretary of the Social Democratic and Labour Party. He was also chair of the United Irishmen Commemoration Society, 1997–8.

AVILA KILMURRAY is director of the Northern Ireland Voluntary Trust and is a founder member of the Northern Ireland Women's Coalition.

MARTIN MANSERGH is head of research for Fianna Fáil and is special adviser to the taoiseach, Bertie Ahern. He held the post of first secretary in the Department of Foreign Affairs in Dublin from 1974 to 1981.

MITCHEL McLAUGHLIN is Sinn Féin's northern chairperson.

MONICA McWILLIAMS is Professor of Women's Studies at the University of Ulster at Jordanstown and is leader of the Northern Ireland Women's Coalition.

DES O'HAGAN is a former lecturer in sociology at Stranmillis College, Belfast. He is currently education officer for the Workers' Party and also sits on its political and executive committees.

# INDEX

abstentionism, 129
accountability
    government, 44
    monarchy, 147
    public, 45
Act of Union (1801), 68, 118, 119, 139
    Repeal movement, 121
active citizenship, 29, 165–167
Adams, Gerry, 25, 72, 73, 74, 110n, 122–123
    Hume–Adams agreement, 73
Addison, Thomas, 142
Adenauer, Konrad, 51, 53
African National Congress, 100
Age of Enlightenment, 151
agreed Ireland, 81
agreed settlement, 74
Ahern, Bertie, 57, 74
allegiance, oaths of, 148–150
Allende, Salvador, 99, 112n
Alliance Party, 3, 9, 56
all-Ireland structures, 83
American Civil War, 49
American colonies, 64
American Constitution *see* United States Constitution
American Declaration of Independence (1776), 34, 44
American National Endowment for Democracy, 101
American Republic, 44
American republicanism, 41–42, 44
American Revolution, 3, 42, 43, 64, 114, 115, 139–140, 157, 158
American War of Independence *see* American Revolution
Amsterdam Treaty, 101
Anderson, Sir John, 108n

Andersonstown (Belfast), 126, 127, 129, 130
Anglo-Irish Treaty (1921), 37–38, 39, 40
Angola, 100
anti-colonial spirit, 17
anti-nationalist republicanism, 17, 18, 23
Antrim
    1798 Rebellion, 116
apathy, 30
Aristotle, 30
armed revolt, 58
armed struggle, 2, 6, 50, 57, 72 *see also* IRA
Armistice Day (1918), 127
Arms Trial (1970), 56
Ascendancy, 43, 65, 67, 115, 118
Asquith, H.H., 69
Auden, W.H., 103

Balkans, 161
BBC, 127
Béaslaí, Piaras, 42
Beattie, Jack, 127
Becket, Thomas à, 133
Belfast, 76
    Andersonstown, 126, 127, 129, 130
    Bombay Street, 131
    Falls Road, 126–127, 130
    La Mon Restaurant bombing, 92
    Rebellion of 1798, 116
    Shankill Road bombings, 91, 92
Belfast Agreement (1998), 25–27, 30
Belfast Harp Festival (1792), 159
*Belfast Telegraph*, 127
Bell, J. Bowyer, 158–159, 160
Benedict, Saint, 132
Bentham, Jeremy, 128
Berlin, Sir Isaiah, 138–139
Bill of Rights (1688), 136–137, 139, 143
Blair government, 104–105

Bloody Friday (July 1972), 92
Bloody Sunday (January 1972), 87
Blundell, John, 111n
Bodenstown, Co. Kildare, 91
Bombay Street (Belfast), 131
Bonaparte, Napoleon, 45, 46
Bonapartism, 119
Boulter, Hugh (Archbishop of Armagh), 65–66
Boundary Agreement (1925), 40, 52
Boundary Commission, 52, 53
Bourbon Restoration, 45
Britain, 7, 16, 20
   disclaimer of any 'selfish, strategic or economic interest', 20, 54, 74–75, 82
British army, 72
British Commonwealth, 38, 50
   united Ireland in association with, 55
British Empire, 35
British government
   talks with Provisionals, 93
   United Irishmen, and, 67–68
British identity, 7, 30, 81
   accommodation of, 17
   one-dimensional approach, 78–80, 81
British interference, 71
British–Irish cooperation, 25, 26
British Labour Party, 104–105, 131
British monarchy. *see* monarchy
British presence, 9
British rule in Ireland, 20, 71 *see also* English rule
British sovereignty in Northern Ireland
   formal recognition of, 26
British Ulster tradition, 10, 160
'Brits out', 94–95, 162, 163
Brookeborough, Lord, 53
BSE crisis, 80
Bunreacht na hÉireann *see* Constitution of Ireland 1937
Burke, Edmund, 47, 108n, 142

Calvin, John, 137–138
Canadian Bill of Rights (1960), 152
capitalism, 104, 105, 112n
Carson, Edward, 35, 37, 69, 70
Casement, Sir Roger, 126
Cathleen ni Houlihan, 167
Catholic community
   legitimisation of Sinn Féin within, 94–96
Catholic Confederates, 42
Catholic culture, 138
Catholic Defenders *see* Defenders
Catholic Emancipation, 118, 139
Catholic middle class, 78
   new nationalism, 97–98
Catholic nationalism, 94
Catholicism, 17
Celtic race, 16
Celtic Tiger, 98
Chambers, John, 116
change, 155
   fear of, 77
   management of, 73, 76
   zero-sum game, 79
Charles I, 42, 134, 136, 145, 146
Chile, 48, 99
Church of England
   disestablishment, 146, 147, 151
Churchill, Winston, 39
CIA, 101
Cicero, Marcus Tullius, 41
citizen power, 9–10, 19, 90–91
citizen self-government, 29–31
citizenship, 29, 150, 158
   active, 29, 162–163, 165–167
   inclusive, 162–165
   oaths of allegiance, and, 149–150
Civic Forum, 29, 166
civic republicanism, 10, 29, 30–31, 158, 159, 161
   challenges of, 162–164
   potential of, 164–168
civic unionism, 161
civic virtues, 31
civil and religious liberty, 43, 122, 161
civil civic relationships, 148
civil rights movement, 50, 87, 90, 108n, 131
   Irish Government's response to, 55–56
civil society, 29
Civil War (England), 135
Civil War, Irish (1922–1923), 7, 39, 70
Clarke, Mrs Tom, 39
Claudy (Co. Derry), 92
Clinton, Bill, 93
   visit to Northern Ireland, 93

# INDEX

co-determination, 26, 57
Cold War, 75
Coleraine (Co. Derry), 92
Collins, Michael, 39, 49, 52
common concerns, 83
common good, 166
common ground, 76–80
common law, 133
Commonwealth (1649), 135
communication problem, 1, 2
community organisations, 94
concept of a republic, 15, 142–143
concept of republicanism, 85
Connolly, James, 37, 86, 126, 128
consent, principle of, 6, 26, 56, 57, 76, 79
Constitution of Ireland (1937), 40, 52, 159, 161
   articles 2 and 3, 26, 40, 153
   Preamble, 152–153
   references to God in, 152–153
   sectarianism in, 111n
constitutional link, 78
constitutional monarchy, 45, 89, 137
constitutional nationalism, 71
constitutional republicanism, 3, 6, 50, 57
   modern nationalism, and, 12, 14
Cook, David, 3, 9, 11, 20, 28
Cooke, Henry, 119
Cope, Sir Alfred, 38
Cosgrave, W.T., 40
Costello, John A., 50
Costello, Seamus, 107n
Craig, William, 108n
Croatian fundamentalists, 107n
Cromwell, Oliver, 120
Cromwellians, 6, 43
Cuba, 99
cultural freedom, 82
cultural nationalism
   republicanism's entanglement with, 16–18
Czech Republic, 104

Dáil Eireann
   Democratic Programme of the first Dáil (1919), 38
   second Dáil, 39, 40
D'Alton, Cardinal, 55
Darkley Pentecostal Church (Co. Armagh), 92

Davis, Thomas, 34, 59
Davitt, Michael, 86, 124
de Gouges, Olympe, 165
De Rossa, Proinsias, 87, 108n
de Valera, Eamon, 6, 35, 38–39, 40, 44, 49–50, 58, 111n, 124–125, 126
   republicanism of, 51–59
de-Anglicisation, 16, 19
Declaration of Independence (1919), 38
Declaration of the Rights of Man and of the Citizen (1789), 45, 140–141, 151, 152
Declaration of the Rights of Woman (1791), 165
Declarations and Resolutions of the Society of United Irishmen of Belfast (1791), 151–152, 154
decommissioning of mindsets, 57
Defenders, 109n, 121, 122, 130
deference, 147–148
democracy, 59, 63, 69, 99
   Calvin's ideas, influence of, 137–138
   daily dialogue, as, 84
democratic deficit, 105
Democratic Left, 87–88, 105
demographic trends, 75–76
Derry (city), 76
Devlin, Joe, 126
devolution, 20, 29, 37, 54, 81
Devoy, John, 35
dialogue, 84
Diana, Princess of Wales, 47, 144
diaspora, 76
difference, politics of, 166
Diggers (1649–1650), 135
direct rule, 73, 99
discrimination, 28, 51, 54, 71
Disraeli, Benjamin, 141
Dissenters, 41
diversity, 114, 136, 154
divided island, 160, 161
divided society, 160, 161
divine right of kings, 103, 134, 144
Donnelly, F., 110n
Down, Co.
   1798 Rebellion, 116
Downing Street Declaration (1993), 57
Dreyfus, Hubert, 4
drugs, 83
Dublin Castle, 122

# INDEX

Dublin Society Of the United Irishmen, 21, 66–67

Easter Rising (1916), 70
  fiftieth anniversary commemoration, 50
  legacy of, 34–40
economic cooperation, 26, 54, 55, 83
Education Act (1947), 98
Edward VIII, 145
Eleanor of Aquitaine, 133
Elisabeth, Empress ('Sissy'), 47
Elizabeth I, 42
Elizabeth II, 127
Elliott, Marianne, 123
emigration, 83
Emmet, Robert, 59, 86, 124
Emmet, Thomas Addis, 116
English interference, 63
English rule
  United Irishmen's opposition to, 9, 19, 20, 82, 123, 158
Enniskillen (Co. Fermanagh)
  war memorial bombing (1987), 92
equality, 133, 135, 139, 140, 143, 148, 154
equality agenda, 7, 83–84
equality legislation, 28
ethnic cleansing, 111n
ethnic supremacy, 16
ethnicity, 167–168
ethno-cultural nationalism, 163
European Commission, 80
European Committee for Peace and Security, 100
European cooperation and integration, 25
European Court, 80
European Parliament, 80
European regionalism, 24–25
European republicanism, 41, 46–48
  French Revolution, 42, 45–46
European Union, 48, 75, 80, 81, 106, 161

Falls Road (Belfast), 126–127, 130
Famine, 95
fascism, 102
federal solution, 51
Fenians, 49, 51, 69, 123
feudal system, 148–149

Fianna Fáil, 3, 39, 40, 53, 56, 57, 101, 108n, 109n, 110n
  pan-nationalist front, and, 93
  republican party, as, 39, 110n–111n
Fine Gael, 39
Fitt, Gerry, 130
FitzGerald, Desmond, 36, 60n
FitzGerald, Lord Edward, 49
FitzGerald, Pamela, 49
flags and emblems, 95
Fontevrault l'Abbaye (France), 132–133, 154–155
foreign influences, 22
Forum for Peace and Reconciliation, 93
Franz Joseph, Emperor of Austria, 47
fraternity, 139
French Constitution, 143, 151
French republicanism, 42, 45–46, 48
French Revolution, 3, 41, 64, 86, 114, 115, 139–140, 157
  monarchy, effect on, 46–47
  republicanism, 45
Friedman, Milton, 111n–112n

GAA, 78, 96
Gaelic football, 96
Gaelic Ireland, 16, 38
Gaelic Irish, 63
Gaelic sport, 96
Gaelicism, 17
Galbraith, J.K., 104, 112n
Garland, Sean, 88, 108n, 112n
general election (1918), 70, 161
George III, 46, 137, 139
George V, 147
German Federal Republic
  Basic Law, 152
Germany, 35, 51
gerrymandering, 52
Gettysburg Address (1863), 44
Gideon, 41
Gildea, Robert, 113
Gilmore, George, 107n
Gladstone, W.E., 139, 149
Glentoran, Lord, 54–55
glorious defeat, myth of, 124
Glorious Revolution, 43
God
  belief in, 150

constitutional references to, 150–153, 154, 155
Goulding, Cathal, 86, 87, 107n
Government of Ireland Act (1920), 51, 161
Grattan, Henry, 59, 115
Gray, John, 125
Greek city-state, 6, 40–41
green card, 14
Grenville, Lord, 65
Griffin, Rev. Victor, 109n
group representation, 166–167
Gustavus, King of Sweden, 46

Habeas Corpus Act (1679), 134
Habermas, Jürgen, 15
Halliday, Fred, 105
Hanna, Eamon, 3, 4, 8, 11, 28
Hattersley, Roy, 104
Havel, Vaclav, 104
Hayes, Maurice, 108n
head of state, 143–144
    ceremonial functions, 144, 146
    hereditary element, 9, 144, 145–146, 147, 154, 155
    president, 144–145
    reform of the monarchy, 146–147
Heaney, Seamus, 128
Henry II, 133, 144
Henry III, 133
Henry VIII, 136
hereditary monarchy *see* monarchy
historic compromise, 81
Hobart, 65
Hoche, Lazare, 45–46
Home Rule, 37, 53, 69
Hope, Jimmy, 117, 125, 128
House of Lords, 47, 147
Hume, John, 24–25, 72, 73, 74, 122
Hume–Adams agreement, 73
hunger strikes (1981), 96, 97
Hutcheson, Francis, 44, 128

Ignatieff, Michael, 161
inclusivism, 17, 18, 19, 74, 164–165
Independent Orange Order, 37
individuality, 138–139
integrated education, 69
internal solution, 73
internationalism, 99–100

internment, 87, 130
Irish Convention (1917–1918), 37
Irish Free State, 16, 39
Irish government, 6
Irish identity, 30, 77–78, 79
Irish language, 78, 95, 116, 127
Irish nation, 16, 17–18
Irish National Liberation Army (INLA), 91, 107n
Irish nationalism *see* nationalism
Irish nationality, 34 *see also* nationality
Irish neutrality, 101
*Irish People*, 101
Irish Protestant tradition, 43
Irish Republic *see* Republic of Ireland
Irish Republican Army (IRA), 53, 73, 86, 158 *see also* Provisional IRA
    Army Council, 107n
    bombing of Britain (1940s), 52, 86
    border campaign (1956–1962), 50, 86, 130
    de Valera's moves against, 53
    modern IRA, 50
Irish Republican Brotherhood (IRB), 49
Irish Republican Socialist Party (IRSP), 91, 93
Irish republicanism, 66
    historical development, 49–59
Irish tricolour, flying of, 95
Irish unity *see* united Ireland
Irish Volunteers, 34, 35, 115, 120
Irish–Americans, 101, 108n, 109n
irredentism, 17, 57
Irregulars, 52
Islamic fundamentalists, 107n

Jacobinism, 164
James II, 42, 43
Japanese Communist Party, 100
Jefferson, Thomas, 44, 46
John, King of England, 133, 134
Johnson, Samuel, 142
Joseph, Emperor of Austria, 46
just society, 155
justice, 135, 139, 140, 143, 148, 154

Kaiser's Germany, 35
Kant, Immanuel, 47–48
Kearney, Richard, 21, 23, 24, 25
Kilmurray, Avila, 3, 10, 11, 28, 29

kingship *see* monarchy
Kingsmills (Co. Armagh), 92
Knox, General, 68
Ku Klux Klan, 102

La Mon Restaurant bombing (Belfast), 92
Labour Government, 104–105
Labour Party, 39
Lake, General, 68
Lalor, James Fintan, 34, 86
legitimation of terrorism, 93–96
Lemass, Seán, 37, 39, 50, 51, 55, 111n
    Oxford Union speech, 54
Lenin, Vladimir Ilyich, 48, 51
Leonard, Tom, 84
Levellers, 120, 135, 141
liberalism, 28, 161
liberty, 37, 139, 140, 156
Lincoln, Abraham, 44
Lloyd George, David, 51, 52, 69
Locke, John, 43
London School of Economics, 105
Louis Napoleon, 45
Louis XV, 47
Louis XVI, 42, 46, 49, 141
Louis-Philippe, 45
loyalists, 79
    terrorist attacks, 109n
Lynch, Liam, 38

Mac Giolla, Tomas, 87, 108n
Mac Stiofáin, Seán, 108n
McAleese, Mary (President of Ireland), 111n
McCartney, Robert, 76
McCracken, Henry Joy, 117, 158
McGuinness, Martin, 110n
Machiavelli, Niccolò, 44
McLaughlin, Mitchel, 3, 6, 8, 14, 17, 23, 28
McNeven, James, 116
MacSwiney, Mary, 38
McWilliams, Monica, 3, 10, 11, 29
Madden, Dr, 117
Magheramorne Manifesto (1905), 37
Magna Carta (1215), 9, 133–134, 143
    Article 39, 134
    Article 54, 135
Maguire, General Thomas, 40

Mansergh, Martin, 3, 5–6, 7, 8, 12, 14, 15, 17, 23, 28
Mansergh, Nicholas, 36
Marie-Antoinette, Queen of France, 47
Markievicz, Countess, 39
Marx, Karl, 48
Mary, Queen of Scots, 42
Mary of Orange, 136–137
Mayhew, Patrick, 54
Maynooth College, 118–119
media, 97
Mellowes, Liam, 86
Middle East, 73
militant nationalism, 56
militant republicanism *see* INLA; IRA; physical force republicanism; Provisional IRA
militarism, rejection of, 86
Mitchel, John, 34, 49, 59
Mitchell Principles, 122
modern Irish nationalism, 12, 14, 57
monarchy, 9, 40–42, 45, 134
    abolition of (1649), 135
    accountability, 147
    Bill of Rights (1688), 136–137
    ceremonial function, 144, 146
    chosen by parliament, 137
    constitutionalisation of, 9, 137, 139
    divine right of kings, 103, 134, 144
    hereditary principle, 9, 144, 145–146, 147, 154, 155
    Queen's Speech, 146
    reform of, 20, 146
    restoration (1660), 43, 136
    succession, 147
Monroe Doctrine for Ireland, 35
Montesquieu, Charles de Secondat, 43
Montgomery, Henry, 119
Moore, Brian, 128
moral force, 125
MPLA Workers' Party (Angola), 100
Mulcahy, Richard, 52
multi-party negotiations (1996–1998), 2, 57

nation
    concept of, 15
    Irish nation, 16
    republic distinguished from, 15
National Democratic Institute, 101

## INDEX

National Democratic Party (NDP), 131
national flag, 49, 95
National Front, 102
national identity, 163
national independence, 11, 157
national question, 5, 10
    pre-occupation with, 11–12
national self-determination *see* self-determination
national sovereignty, 9, 124
national unity *see* united Ireland
nationalisation, 104
nationalism, 6, 101–102
    anti-colonial spirit and, 17
    anti-nationalist republicanism, 17, 18, 23
    cultural nationalism, 16–18
    historic compromise with unionism, 81
    meaning of, 22
    modern Irish nationalism, 12, 14, 57
    nationality and, distinction between, 22–24
    non-threatening, 23
    pan-nationalism, 93
    pro-nationalist republicans, 18, 23
    racism, 102
    republican critique of, 98–103
    republicanism and, 2, 8, 10–11, 11–27, 156–157, 159
    sectarian Roman Catholic nationalism, 94
    Sinn Féin – the new nationalism?, 97–98
    social democracy and Northern nationalism, 113–118
nationalist consensus, 6, 7, 72–74
nationalist expansionism, 102
nationalist fundamentalism, 107n
nationalist majorities, 75
Nationalist Party, 129
nationalist regalia, display of, 78
nationalists, 72 *see also* Northern nationalists
    common ground with unionists, 76–80
    legitimation of terrorism, 93
    separate development, 93–94
nationality
    meaning of, 22–23
    nationalism and, distinction between, 22–24
    republicanism tied to, 26–27
nation-state, 15, 159–160, 161
    out-datedness of, 24, 25
NATO, 101
Nazism, 102, 107n
Neilson, Samuel, 117, 118, 158
neo-Nazis, 102
New Ireland Forum, 69, 111n
New Light Movement, 119
new nationalism, 97–98
Newtownhamilton, Co. Armagh, 92
Nicholas II, Tsar, 42
Noraid, 101
North–South arrangements, 26
North–South cooperation, 26, 54, 55, 58, 83
North–South dimension, 56
Northern assembly, 20, 26, 29
Northern Ireland, 1, 70, 86, 89, 155, 160, 161
    active citizenship, 165–166
    British sovereignty, recognition of, 26
    constitutional position, 11–12, 13
    demographic trends, 75–76
    'failed entity', as, 89–90
    one-party unionist rule, 71, 72
    unionist state for a unionist population, 71–72
Northern Ireland Civil Rights Association (NICRA), 87, 90
Northern Ireland Labour Party, 131
Northern Ireland Women's Coalition, 3, 10, 170
Northern nationalists, 71–72, 89
    increase in population, 75
    Irish identity, 77–78, 79
    social democracy and, 113–118
*Northern Star*, 117, 123, 125
Nussbaum, Martha, 21, 22

Ó Catháin, Ciarán, 130–131
oaths of allegiance, 148–150
obstacles to understanding, 58
O'Connell, Daniel, 119, 120–121, 128
    Repeal movement, 121
O'Donovan Rossa, Jeremiah, 49
O'Hagan, Des, 3, 4, 7, 11, 18, 23, 28

O'Higgins, Bernardo, 48
O'Neill, Hugh, 63–64
O'Neill, Terence, 50, 55
Orange Order, 43, 110n, 114 *see also* Independent Orange Order
    establishment of, 121
    sectarianism, 121
Orangeism, 52
O'Toole, Fintan, 109n

Paine, Thomas, 41, 162
Paisley, Rev. Ian, 76
Palestine Liberation Organisation (PLO), 100
pan-nationalism, 93
paramilitarism, 122–125
parliamentary democracy, 137
parliamentary reform, 67, 82, 141
Parnell, Charles Stewart, 34, 59
participative politics, 166
partition of Ireland, 20, 70
    consequences of, 6–7, 70–71
    ending of, 5, 11, 13, 14, 53, 54, 86
    failure of, 74
partitionism, 161–162
peace process, 93
    Hume–Adams agreement, 73
Pearse, Patrick, 34, 35, 36, 37, 39, 49, 51, 121, 123, 124, 126
Peep o'Day Boys, 109n
Penal Laws, 136
Petition of Right (1628), 134
Pettit, Philip, 156, 162, 167
Philippe-Egalité, Duke of Orléans, 49
physical force republicanism, 4, 68, 125, 126, 130, 131 *see also* INLA; IRA; Provisional IRA
    futility of military campaigns, 86
physical union, 80, 81
Pitt, William (The Younger), 119, 139
Plato, 41
pluralism, 7, 9–10, 28, 136, 138, 152, 154, 155
Poland, 48
political alienation, 30
political consensus, 76
political ethics, 91
political legitimacy, 93, 123
political participation, 29, 30
political power, 19

political priorities, 10
political progress, 62
political union, 80
post-nationalist Ireland, 23
post-nationalist republicanism, 168
post-nationalist world, 25
Powell, Enoch, 114
power-sharing, 26, 56
Presbyterians, 42, 64, 65, 119–120, 128–129, 138
    radicalism, 120
    republicanism, espousal of, 119, 120
    Ulster Presbyterianism, 42, 119–120
    United Irish movement, involvement in, 66, 116, 121, 125
Proclamation of the Irish Republic (1916), 34, 36–37, 38, 153–154, 161
    self-determination, 37
pro-nationalist republicans, 18, 23
property rights, 133
Protestant Ascendancy *see* Ascendancy
Protestant culture, 138
Protestant tradition, 43
Protestant/unionist community *see also* unionists
    historical options of, 59
    republican murders of members of, 91–92, 109n
Provisional Alliance, 87, 108n, 110n
Provisional IRA, 8, 91, 107n, 109n
    1969–1994 campaign, 56, 58, 72, 87, 90, 91–92
    cessation of military activities (August 1994), 73
    foundation (1970), 87
    motivation, 90
    right-wing Irish-American organisations, and, 101
    sectarian murders carried out by, 91–92
Provisional symbolism, 95–96
Provisionalism, 90
purist attitude, 11

Quesnay, Dr, 47

Randalstown (Co. Antrim), 116
Rebellion of 1798, 68, 81, 113–115, 125, 128 *see also* United Irishmen
    Antrim and Down, 116

# INDEX

Belfast, 116
bicentenary commemorations, 113–114
casualties, 68
Northern Catholics, role of, 116
Wexford, 49, 116
Reform Bill (1832), 141
regions, 25
religion, practice of, 151
religious fundamentalism, 107n
religious tolerance, 45, 46
Representation of the People Act (1918), 162
representative parliamentary democracy, 142
republic
   concept of, 15, 142–143
   ideal republic, 154
   nation, distinguished from, 15
   pluralist state, 154
Republic of Ireland, 86, 89, 161
   Constitution *see* Constitution of Ireland
   ethos alien to unionism and Protestantism, 16, 17
   formal declaration (1949), 50
   national pride, 58
   partitionism, 161–162
   pluralist society, 17
   President, 145
   soccer team, 78
   territorial claim, 26
Republican Clubs, 157
Republican Congress, 86, 87, 107n, 163
republican constitutions, 140–141
republican ethic, 90–91
republican freedom, 156
republican goal, 84, 86
   ending of partition, 11, 13, 18, 86
republican ideology, 89
republican imperatives, 88–90
republican maxims, 45–46
republican movement, 107n *see also* INLA; IRA; Provisional IRA; Republican Sinn Féin; Sinn Féin
   legitimist thread, 40
   review of Workers' Party development, 86–88
republican-nationalist alliance, 14
republican parties, 40 *see also* Fianna Fáil; Sinn Féin; Workers' Party
republican sectarian murders, 91–92
Republican Sinn Féin, 40, 165
republican socialism, 52
republican society, 28–32
republicanism, 135 *see also* civic republicanism; constitutional republicanism
   American Republic, 44
   American Revolution, 41–42
   citizen power, 9–10
   citizen self-government, 29–31
   compatibility with British nationalism, 12
   Cromwellians, 6, 43
   cultural nationalism, 16
   de Valera republicanism and its subsequent evolution, 51–59
   distortions of, 2
   eighteenth-century origins, 3
   Europe, in, 48
   exclusive nationalist tendencies, 12, 18
   French Revolution, 42, 45–46
   historical and international perspective, 40–48
   historical legacy, 157–160
   ideological critique of nationalism, 98–103
   inclusivism, 17
   Irish republicanism from the 1790s, 49–59
   nationalism and, 2, 8, 10–11, 11–27, 156–157, 159
   new republicanism, 24–25
   non-sectarian, democratic and inclusive, 10
   Plato's ideal republic, 41
   post-nationalist, 168
   Presbyterianism's espousal of, 119, 120
   sectarianism, and, 2
   United Irishmen *see* United Irishmen
   violence, and, 2 *see also* physical force republicanism
   Workers' Party programme, 98–101
respect for fellow citizens, 148
responsibilities, 82
revisionism, 56–57, 116–117, 162
Reynolds, Albert, 72, 73, 74

Richard I, 133
rights, 82, 83
rituals, 96
Romans, 15, 41
Rousseau, Jean Jacques, 43–44, 166
Royal Belfast Academical Institution, 120
royal family, 146
rule of law, 45, 133, 135
Russell, Thomas, 66, 125, 158
Russia, 48
Russian Revolution (1917), 105, 142

sacrifice, 95–96
St Malachy's College (Belfast), 127
Sampson, William, 116
Samuel, 41
Sandel, Michael, 31
Santayana, George, 126
Scottish devolution, 81
sectarian nationalism, 2, 94
sectarian violence, 8, 91–92
sectarianism, 2, 7, 8, 28, 67, 69, 71, 79, 99, 121–122, 136
   cultural nationalism and, 17
   Irish Constitution, in, 111n
   Orange Order, 121
   republican sectarian murders, 91–92
   Tone's refusal to submit to, 91
self-determination, 6, 7, 27, 48, 57, 71, 73, 74, 102, 159, 161, 163
   co-determination, replaced by, 26
   Proclamation of 1916, 37
self-governing cities, 41
self-government by citizens, 29–31
separate nationalist development, 93–94
separatism, 9, 123, 124, 158
   Irish Catholic nationalism, identified with, 119
Shakespeare, William, 41
Shankill Road bombings, 91, 92
Simms brothers, 158
Sinn Féin, 3, 4, 6, 7, 8, 25, 37, 39, 40, 51, 70, 74, 86, 87, 93, 94, 95, 96, 97–98, 107n, 114, 129, 131, 165
   absorption into the constitutional process, 93
   abstentionism, 129–130
   analysis of, 74
   Catholic middle-class vote, 97
   dialogue with SDLP, 72
   electoral gains, 97–98, 110n
   legitimisation of, 94–96
   new nationalism, 97–98
   SDLP vote transfers to, 94
   separate nationalist development, 93–94
   US Administration and, 93
Sinn Féin – the Workers' Party, 107n
slavery, 158
Social and Democratic Labour Party (SDLP), 3, 6, 8, 56, 93, 94, 97, 130, 131
   dialogue with Sinn Féin, 72
   transfer of voting preferences to Sinn Féin, 94
social and political apartheid, 71
social and political life, quality of, 13
social democracy
   Northern nationalism, and, 113–118
socialism, 28, 52, 108n, 111n
   jettisoning of socialist ideology, 104–105
Society of United Irishmen *see* United Irishmen
South Africa, 73, 100, 102
sovereignty of the people, 57
Soviet experiment, 112n
Spanish Republic, 107n
Stalin, Joseph, 111n
Stewart, A.T.Q., 124
Stormont elections, 129
Stormont Parliament, 124
Stormont regime, 39, 55, 71, 73, 76, 127
   civil rights challenge to, 55
strategic interests, 74–75
Stuart restoration, 43
Swift, Jonathan, 42, 59, 131
Switzerland, 41
symbols, 95

Tawney, R.H., 104
Taylor, Charles, 24, 25
Teebane (Co. Tyrone)
   bombing of workers' van (1992), 92
Teeling, Bartholomew, 116
terrorism
   legitimation of, 93–96
   loyalist terrorists, 109n
   republican sectarian murders, 91–92

# INDEX

Thatcher, Margaret, 111n
*Times* (London), 104, 134
tolerance, 154
Tone, Theobald Wolfe, 34, 36, 45, 51, 59, 86, 88, 90, 114, 117, 126, 128, 157
   *An Argument on Behalf of the Catholics of Ireland*, 66
   central messages, 109n
   citizenship, and, 109n, 158
   civic republicanism, 158, 162
   Declarations and Resolutions of the Society of United Irishmen of Belfast (1791), 151–152, 154
   sectarianism, and, 91
   self-critical challenge, 42–43
   separatist cause, 123, 158
   unity of 'Protestant, Catholic and Dissenter', 10, 16, 50–51, 91, 109n, 124, 158, 160, 168
tourism, 54
tricolour, flying of, 95

Ulster Presbyterians, 119–120 *see also* Presbyterians
   loyalty of, questioned by James II, 42
Ulster Unionist Party, 129 *see also* unionists
Ulster Volunteer Force (UVF), 35
*Union Doctrine or a Poor Man's Catechism, The*, 141, 151
union with Britain, 68–69, 81
   Act of Union (1801), 68, 118, 119, 121, 139
   unionist sense of identity and, 77, 78
unionist identity, 55
   one-dimensional approach to, 78–80, 81
unionist politics, 79
unionist violence, 71
unionists, 11, 12, 50, 59, 65
   common ground with nationalists, 76–80
   declining population, 75
   historic compromise with nationalism, 81
   historical options of, 59
   lackeys of a colonial power, seen as, 17
   loyalists, 79, 109n
   majority rule, 52
   one-party unionist rule, 71, 72
united Ireland, 8, 11, 18, 19, 20, 50, 54, 55, 58, 73, 86, 122, 160
   changing British government policy, 77
   Commonwealth, associated with, 55
   convincing unionists of merits of, 77
   nationalist belief in, 76–77
United Irishmen, 4, 69, 84, 86, 90, 113–118, 119, 120, 121, 126, 128, 130 *see also* Rebellion of 1798; Tone, Theobald Wolfe
   anti-Orange propaganda, 49
   anti-sectarian ideal, 17, 67
   British government coercion, 67–68
   constitution, 66
   corruption of ideal of, 16
   criticisms of, 116–117, 120–121
   Declarations and Resolutions of the Society of United Irishmen of Belfast (1791), 151–152, 154
   English rule, opposition to, 9, 19, 20, 82, 123, 158
   founding of, 66–67, 114
   generosity of heart, 125
   guiding principles, 81–82
   internationalism, 124, 128
   Irish Catholic nationalism's co-option of, 124
   Irish language publications, 115–116
   nationalism and, 18–19
   non-sectarian politics, 17, 20, 67, 82, 114, 116, 118
   O'Connell's anathematisation of, 120–121
   paramilitarism, and, 122
   parliamentary reform, 67, 82
   physical force, and, 68, 125
   policies and ideas, 141, 151
   Presbyterian involvement, 66, 116, 121, 125
   republicanism of, 3, 6, 7, 8, 10, 23, 123
   sectarianism, 122
   separatism, 158, 162
   social agenda, 117–118
   *Union Doctrine*, 141, 151
   universal dimension, 21, 22, 23–24
   vision of, 114–115
United States, 21–22, 44, 101, 102, 104

*see also* Irish-Americans
President, 144
welcome for Sinn Féin leaders, 93
United States Constitution, 134, 140–141, 143, 151
unity of 'Protestant, Catholic and Dissenter'
Tone's vision of, 10, 16, 50–51, 91, 109n, 124, 158, 160, 168
universalism, 21, 22, 23, 24
University College Dublin, 51

Vietnam, 100
violence, 1–2, 11, 53, 56, 122–125, 161–162 *see also* physical-force republicanism
loyalists, 109n
militant nationalism, 56
paramilitarism, 122–125
republican sectarian murders, 91–92
Ulster unionists, by, 71

wall murals, 95–96
Walzer, Michael, 21, 22
War of Independence (1919–1921), 35, 38, 70, 86
Warden, David Bailie, 116
Wellington, Duke of, 141

Welsh devolution, 81
Westminster Parliament, 81
Wexford Rising (1798), 49, 116
Wilde, Oscar, 115
William of Orange, 43, 136–137
William the Silent, 43
Williamite Wars, 118
Wilson, Woodrow, 48
Women's Coalition *see* Northern Ireland's Women's Coalition
women's movement, 10, 164–165
women's suffrage, 162
Workers' Party, 3, 7, 96, 97, 98, 99, 100, 101, 157
goal of, 98–99
international activity, 99–100
philosophical development, 85–88
working-class unity, 8
world citizenship, 21
World War I, 35, 48
World War II, 53, 86, 102

Yeats, William Butler, 37, 59
Young, Iris, 166
Young Ireland movement, 49, 69, 121

zero-sum conundrum, 77, 79